The DeFiore Brothers

A brand-new duet by Jennifer Faye!

A recipe for dating DeFiore men...

*Take two Italian brothers
with a pinch of playboy charm.*

*Add two American sisters
with a liberal dash of feistiness.*

*Simmer under warm Italian skies
until perfectly combined.*

Serve with lashings of love.

To start: *The Playboy of Rome*

Dante DeFiore is passionate about life, women and the tasty Italian food he creates. With the arrival of feisty American TV star Lizzie Addler, he finds her almost too tempting to resist! As the temperature soars in the kitchen, the passion between Lizzie and Dante simmers until they reach boiling point. Has this Italian playboy finally met his match?

The main: *Best Man for the Bridesmaid*

Stefano DeFiore is proud and reserved—he likes the quiet life. So planning a wedding for his celebrity chef brother is his idea of hell. But when bold and colorful Jules Lane enters his world—chief bridesmaid and sister to the bride—Stefano decides to take his best man duties seriously...including doing all he can to make Jules's time in Italy simply heaven...

To finish: Happily-ever-after?

Dear Reader,

Sometimes being unique isn't so much a voluntary choice but rather something that is thrust upon you—something you might not have chosen for yourself if given a choice. Sometimes you camouflage those differences and sometimes you flaunt them.

Jules Lane is a girl who marches to her own drummer—from her black platform knee-high boots to her black and purple wardrobe, her distinctive eye makeup and her pigtails. She doesn't care what people think of her appearance. *She* likes it. Oh, and did I mention her little purple butterfly tattoo?

But in walks Stefano DeFiore—a tall, dark and some might say conservative man. He's lived his whole life on his family's sprawling vineyard and he's shut himself off from the world since his wife's tragic death. So when he comes face-to-face with his younger brother's soon-to-be sister-in-law, he isn't sure what to make of her. *Oh, men.* He has a lot to learn, and Jules is just the person to teach him.

With wedding bells chiming for Jules's sister and Stefano's brother, romance is in the air. Will Jules let down her guard and allow Stefano to see the real woman hiding behind the clothes and the makeup? And will Stefano allow his eyes to be opened to the life that's awaiting him if he can allow himself to live again?

Join Jules and Stefano as they prepare for a festive vineyard wedding.

Happy reading!

Jennifer

Best Man for the Bridesmaid

Jennifer Faye

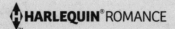

HARLEQUIN® ROMANCE

Recycling programs
for this product may
not exist in your area.

ISBN-13: 978-0-373-74334-6

Best Man for the Bridesmaid

First North American Publication 2015

Copyright © 2015 by Jennifer F. Stroka

HHARLEQUIN®

www.Harlequin.com

Printed in U.S.A.

Award-winning author **Jennifer Faye** pens fun, heartwarming romances. Jennifer has won the *RT Book Reviews* Reviewers' Choice Award, is a Top Pick author and has been nominated for numerous awards. Now living her dream, she resides with her patient husband, one amazing daughter (the other remarkable daughter is off chasing her own dreams) and two spoiled cats. She'd love to hear from you via her website, jenniferfaye.com.

Books by Jennifer Faye

HARLEQUIN ROMANCE

Rancher to the Rescue
Snowbound with the Soldier
Safe in the Tycoon's Arms
The Return of the Rebel
A Princess by Christmas

The DeFiore Brothers

The Playboy of Rome

Visit the Author Profile page
at Harlequin.com for more titles

For Linda.

To an amazing lady
who has a heart as big as Texas.

Thanks for your guidance and support
over the years. This one is for you!

CHAPTER ONE

Jules Lane lifted her chin and smiled broadly.

Her steps grew quicker as she made her way past the other departing passengers. At last she was in Rome. Rome, Italy, to be exact. She continued to grin and resisted the urge to pinch herself just to make sure this wasn't a dream.

On the other hand, this wasn't exactly a vacation. She was here for an important job—to help plan her foster sister's wedding. This wouldn't be Jules's first time down the aisle. She'd been a bridesmaid more times than she could count on one hand.

However, this time around she had the privilege of being the maid of honor. It was a role she eagerly anticipated. She liked to take charge—to provide order to chaos. She wasn't a closet romantic. She didn't dream about finding Prince Charming. She didn't fantasize about her "big day." But she did have a thing for pretty dresses and cake—cake was definitely her weakness.

Actually now that she thought about it, Lizzie, her foster sister, hadn't been into romance, either…at least not until she'd flown here three months ago for a television show—a reality segment about cooking. Cupid sure seemed to have hit the mark with Lizzie and Dante.

For most of Jules's life, Lizzie had been the keeper of her secrets, her protector and her only family. Jules loved her with all her heart. But that security came with a steep price tag for both of them—learning at an early age that they only had each other to lean on.

Now it was time for a change—if only Jules could find a way to tell Lizzie her news.

Jules sighed as she made her way through the Leonardo da Vinci terminal. She'd find the right time. She just had to have patience.

The strap of her carry-on dug into her shoulder, and she struggled to adjust it. The black-and-white cloth bag was weighted down with a wedding planner, a big bag of sour candies and plenty of bridal magazines with dog-eared pages and sticky notes. She had everything necessary to plan the perfect wedding—except for one very important but necessary ingredient: caffeine. But no worries—Lizzie had been raving about the delicious coffee Rome had to offer.

Considering no details about the wedding had been tacked down, there would be long conversations over this now-infamous coffee. First, they had to nail down a wedding date. Jules was thinking a spring wedding next year. It'd be perfect as Lizzie had mentioned something about an Italian vineyard as the backdrop. Talk about some amazing photos.

This wedding-planning stuff shouldn't be too hard. After all, Jules had most of it memorized by this point. Now she'd be able to put all of that knowledge to good use.

Boisterous voices filled the terminal as friends greeted each other. An American family called frantically for their son, who stood ten steps away checking out the cell phones that a beautiful woman with long dark hair and a brilliant smile was eager to show the teenager. Jules took it all in as she strode through the congested concourse, following the signs to the baggage claim.

She couldn't wait to see Lizzie. It felt like an eternity since they'd seen each other. And she was looking forward to meeting her future brother-in-law, Dante. Lizzie swore the photos she'd emailed didn't do him justice. That was hard to believe since Jules had found him quite handsome.

She walked over to the luggage carousel, hoping her suitcase had made the journey and hadn't been lost along the way. All the while, she kept glancing around for Lizzie. Where could she be? It wasn't like her to be late.

Jules's gaze strayed across to a tall dark-haired man at the other end of the luggage return area. He spoke to a pretty young woman, who shook her head and turned away. And then he moved on to the next young woman. What was that all about?

Jules shrugged and turned away. She pulled the phone from her pocket, hoping a message from Lizzie would pop up, but instead a dead battery symbol flashed on the screen and then everything went black. Jules sighed. This couldn't be happening to her while she was all alone in a foreign country. She'd charged it before she left New York, hadn't she?

"*Scusi.* Are you Ms. Lane?" A deep male voice immediately drew her attention.

She turned to find the same dark-haired man speaking to a woman a couple of people down from her. Was he looking for her? How did he know her name?

When the blonde woman wearing a pastel flowered dress shook her head, he moved on. He skipped over an older woman, not even bothering to ask her. And then his gaze skimmed over Jules's pigtails, long-sleeved black top, purple-and-black plaid miniskirt and knee-high platform black boots. His facial expression remained neutral, but he didn't say a word to her as he moved on down the line.

Seriously? He was that put off by her appearance that he wasn't even going to speak to her? She turned her back to him. Then she realized he might have a message from Lizzie. Jules turned back around.

He stopped at the next young woman. "*Scusi,* are you Julianne—"

"Hey, mister." When he turned to her with a raised brow, she had to fight back a laugh. "I'm Julianne Lane."

He apologized to the young lady before backtracking and stopping directly in front of Jules. His forehead was creased. "*Signorina,* you are Lizzie's sister?"

She nodded. Her pigtails bobbed. He wasn't the first person to be surprised by her unconventional appearance. She'd given up a long time ago trying to live up to everyone's expectations. And she'd been dressing this way so long now that it came naturally.

The same couldn't be said about him. He looked as if he'd just walked off the cover of a men's fashion magazine. His navy blue suit was perfectly tailored to show off his broad shoulders, and the gray dress shirt was unbuttoned just enough to show off a hint of his muscular chest.

Jules swallowed hard. *Wow!* No wonder Lizzie lost her heart here. They sure made them hot and sexy in Italy.

With effort, she forced her gaze upward to meet his serious stare. "Is there a problem?"

"Umm…no." The lines on his forehead smoothed. "Lizzie is your sister, isn't she?"

Jules's chest tightened. "Yes. Is she all right?"

His dark brows rose as his warm brown eyes seemed to hold her captive. "Yes, she is."

Jules breathed out a pent-up breath. "Don't do that."

"Do what?"

"Scare me. I thought something had happened to my sister."

"I assure you that she's perfectly fine. But something came up and she asked me to pick you up."

"You should have said that part first." She glanced over at the luggage carousel, which had started to move. Before she could ask him anymore questions, the luggage appeared on the conveyer belt. "I'll be right with you. I just need to grab my bag."

She could feel the man's curious gaze boring into her back. She wondered what he was thinking, but something told her she was better off not knowing.

And then her black suitcase with the large white circle pattern dropped onto the conveyer belt. She shifted her carry-on so that it was resting against her back and out of her way to grab the large piece of luggage.

As she reached for it, the man stepped between her and the belt. "Let me grab that for you. Which is it?"

"Don't bother. I've got it." She didn't need him going out of his way for her. She wasn't some spoiled rich girl. Not by anyone's imagination. She'd been taking care of herself for a long time. Maybe that's what always scared men off. She didn't need them.

The man's eyes widened as he backed away. "Ms. Lane, I only meant to help."

She grabbed the suitcase and swung it around to place it on the floor beside her. "I appreciate your offer, but I'm used to taking care of myself. And, by the way, I prefer to go by Jules. Who would you be?"

"I'm Stefano DeFiore. Dante's older brother."

Lizzie had mentioned in passing that Dante had a brother, but she'd never mentioned how good-looking he was or that he would be meeting her at the airport. "Nice to meet you."

She smiled and stuck out her hand. He hesitated for a moment before glancing quickly to the left and then to the right before his hand encased hers. Was he looking around to see if anyone noticed that he hadn't gotten her luggage for her?

Really? He was that worried about what everyone thought?

And then the smile slipped from her face. Her stomach plummeted. She realized the real reason for his awkwardness. He was embarrassed to be seen with her.

What kind of family was Lizzie marrying into?

Stefano DeFiore found himself utterly mesmerized—and that was something that he never let happen.

He struggled to keep his gaze anywhere but on the delicate tiny blue—or was it purple?—butterfly body art flirting with the beginning of the swell of her breasts…just above the diving neckline of her black top. He found it and her absolutely fascinating. And that was not good.

He swallowed hard and drew his focus back up to her face. His brother and his soon-to-be sister-in-law should have picked up Jules—not him. But family takes care of family.

Jules was undeniably intriguing but not in the usual manner. Her goth style was unique, to say the least. And then there was the purplish lipstick, heavy black eyeliner and the stuff on her eyelashes that set off her look. He was anxious to see the woman beneath it all.

He certainly didn't know what to make of Julianne—erm—Jules. Lizzie hadn't given any hints that her sister was so different from her in every way. Lizzie was tall, fair and blonde; Jules was the opposite. She was shorter in stature with dark brown hair in twin ponytails and long sweeping bangs that she brushed off to the side.

Realizing he was staring, he said, "We should get moving. Lizzie should be done with her meeting when we get there."

"Get where?" Jules eyed him as though she wasn't planning to budge.

She didn't trust him. It was a new experience for him. There had been a time in his life when he didn't have a problem putting the female persuasion at ease. But he wasn't exactly acting like the old smooth-talking guy he used to be. Things had changed a lot in recent years.

Combine that with his concerns over his younger brother's sudden wedding announcement and the fact that he'd been elected to play chauffeur today without so much as waiting for him to agree and he was left feeling out of sorts.

Stefano swallowed down his agitation and tried to soften his tone. "I'm dropping you off at Dante's place, Ristorante Massimo. It's not that far from here."

She gave him one last hard look as though making up her mind about him. "Sounds like a plan. Let's get moving."

He reached for her suitcase but then hesitated,

recalling how she'd expressed her desire to remain independent. He returned his hand to his side as she extended the handle on her luggage. He merely shook his head and turned away. His lack of understanding where women were concerned had cost him dearly not so long ago. Since then he'd learned to refrain from flirting with them. Relationships were a thing of the past for him.

So then why did he find Jules so intriguing? He couldn't help casting her the occasional glance. It had to be her pigtails. Did grown women really wear those? He smiled. They did look cute on her.

But it was the butterfly that kept him distracted. He pictured it in his mind's eye. He had to admit that he'd never been intrigued by a tattoo before. His late wife had had a fear of needles, so getting any sort of body art wasn't even a possibility. And they'd lived out in the country where that sort of thing wasn't popular in the nearby village.

When his shoulder collided with someone, he glanced up. *"Scusi."*

He could feel Jules's gaze on him, but he pretended not to notice. He wasn't about to let on that her little butterfly had him distracted to the point of not watching where he was walking. After all, he was a DeFiore. DeFiores didn't allow themselves to be distracted.

Once they were situated in his sleek black luxury sedan, which he only used when escorting around special guests of the DeFiore Vineyard, he turned to Jules. Her body was stiff and her hands were clasped in her lap. He supposed that was to be expected. He hadn't exactly made her feel welcome. He really needed to try harder. After all, it was important to Dante that this visit go well.

Stefano was about to say something when that darn butterfly once again snagged his attention. It rose and fell with her every breath. He was being ridiculous. It was just an inconsequential tattoo—that teased and taunted him.

He turned and stared blindly out the windshield. "Is this your first trip to Rome?"

"Yes, it is." Jules turned to him, but he kept his gaze directly ahead. "What happened? I mean, Lizzie was supposed to pick me up."

"She didn't tell you?"

"No. My phone battery died, so I haven't been able to talk to her."

This was his chance to see what Jules thought of the impending nuptials. He was curious to see if she thought they were a bit rushed. "When Dante called, he said that the announcement of their engagement made a big splash with the paparazzi, and the studio heads wanted to figure out how to work the wedding into an upcoming show."

"What does their wedding have to do with a cooking show?"

"My thoughts exactly. Maybe it'll delay the wedding."

"Why would you say that?" Suspicion laced every syllable.

This is where he had to move carefully. He sensed Jules's defenses kicking into gear, and he didn't blame her. He'd react the same way if he thought someone was about to jeopardize his brother's happiness.

Again Jules's taunting butterfly came to mind as well as her different taste in clothes. Something told him that she wasn't a traditionalist like his family was. Maybe she was one of those live-on-a-whim types? Even if it meant letting people set themselves up to get hurt?

Like he'd done to himself.

Like he'd done to his late wife.

CHAPTER TWO

THE SILENCE STRETCHED OUT.

The longer it took Stefano to answer her, the more concerned Jules became. With her sister's happiness at stake, Jules couldn't let the subject drop. Not without some answers.

She turned in her seat in order to gauge Stefano's expression. "Why do you want them to delay the wedding?"

He sighed. "I just think they are rushing into this without thinking it through."

"It sounds to me like you're opposed to the wedding." Jules sank back against the leather seat. Surely she had to be jet-lagged and reading too much into his reserved demeanor and hesitant words. Perhaps she needed to be more direct. "Will you try and stop the wedding?"

Jules studied his handsome face with its aristocratic features for some indication of his thoughts. Because there was no way she'd let anyone come between Lizzie and her happiness. Over the years, when they'd fantasized about the future, Lizzie had always dreamed of meeting Mr. Right. But neither of them had ever invested much hope in those dreams. Until now. This was Lizzie's chance to live out her dream.

Though that meant breaking up their small family and the thought saddened Jules, she refused to dwell on it. Lizzie's happiness had to be the priority. And on a positive note, this meant Jules would at last gain her freedom to make all her own choices. They'd been making decisions together since they were kids, but now it was time they each stood on their own. And for Jules that meant making her own career choice—one Lizzie wouldn't approve of.

And if Jules was ready to see her foster sister—her only family—move an ocean away so that she would be happy, what possible reason could Stefano find to object to the wedding? Or was she reading him wrong? It was so hard to tell—his tanned face wasn't giving her any clues about his thoughts.

"I'm waiting for an explanation." She crossed her arms. No way was she going to drop the subject until they sorted it out.

"Fine. I'll admit it. I'm not a fan of marriage."

"This particular marriage? Or just marriage in general?" She could have sworn that Lizzie had mentioned he was married. Maybe that was it. Maybe he and his wife had hit a rough patch. "Aren't you married?"

"I was." His knuckles on the steering wheel gleamed white. "She died."

"Oh. Sorry." *Great job, Jules. Talk about opening your mouth and inserting your size-six boot.*

"And for the record, it's not my place to say whether the wedding should go on or not. My brother has a mind of his own."

"Good." She settled back against the smoky-gray leather seat. "I don't want anything ruining this wedding for them." She gave him a pointed look, but Stefano didn't give her the satisfaction of looking her way. "We have a lot to plan between now and next spring or summer. Have they mentioned to you if they've picked a date?"

"No. But it sounded to me like it is going to be sooner than next year."

"They can't move up the wedding. That would be a nightmare. There's just too much to arrange. Besides, if they were doing something like that, they'd have told us. After all, you're the best man."

Stefano sighed. "I suppose I am. But that just means they'll tell me when and where to show up."

"You really think you'll get off that easily?"

"Why wouldn't I? Men don't care about all of that stuff. Weddings are for women."

"We'll see about that." Did he really believe that? Was he that jaded? Or was it grief over losing his wife?

"I guess we will."

She pressed her lips firmly together. She'd been in Rome less than an hour. It wouldn't do to wage war with Lizzie's future brother-in-law.

Jules inhaled a deep, calming breath and noticed the very fine automobile had a wonderful new car scent. Her gaze strayed to the dash, where Stefano's long, lean fingers were adjusting the controls on a large touch screen. Soon the velvet sounds of an Italian baritone replaced the oppressive silence.

She leaned her head back and turned to the window. She took in the golden glow of the sun over the city. People were out and about—neighbors filling each other in on the events of the day. Children were running around laughing and playing. Jules smiled, liking what she'd seen so far.

She couldn't believe that she was truly in Italy. Her friends back at the New York City coffee shop where she worked were never going to believe this. She'd definitely have to get lots of photos before catching her flight in a week.

When the car pulled to a stop, Stefano turned to her. "We're here."

So this was Ristorante Massimo.

Jules stared out the window at the line of patio tables with red umbrellas. And the double red doors with large brass handles that led to the dining area. This was where her sister had lost her heart—this was where Lizzie intended to spend the rest of her life.

The breath caught in Jules's throat. She might at last be gaining her freedom, but at what cost? She blinked repeatedly. She'd told herself the whole flight here that she wouldn't melt into a sobbing mess.

A hand pressed against her shoulder. "Julianne... um, Jules, are you okay?"

She nodded and blinked, tucking her emotions into that trusty box she'd been using since the days of being shuttled in and out of foster homes. She swallowed down the lump in her throat, hoping that when she spoke her voice wouldn't waver. "I'm fine."

"Why don't you go inside? I'm sure Lizzie is anxious to see you. I'll grab your luggage and meet you in there."

She agreed and made her way inside. The restaurant was quite large, and a wall of photos was the first thing to grab her attention. There were framed photos of various sizes and all manner of frames starting at the ceiling and trailing down to the floor. As she passed by, she noticed some famous faces. *Wow! This place must be really upscale.*

"Jules, is that you?" Lizzie came rushing toward her.

In no time, they were wrapped in each other's arms. It felt so good to be with her sister again. They both started to talk at once. It wasn't until they glanced around and saw Dante and Stefano observing them with amusement dancing in their eyes that both women realized their lack of manners.

Lizzie stepped in the middle of everyone. "Jules, I'd like you to meet Dante, my future husband. Dante, this is my sister, Julianne, but everyone calls her Jules."

"Hello, Jules."

"Hi." When she went to hold her hand out to him to shake, he pulled her forward and gave her a big hug.

She hesitated at first. This wasn't the sort of greeting she was accustomed to. It certainly wasn't the sort of greeting she'd received from Stefano. When Dante let her go, she gazed up at him. He was almost as tall as Stefano. But he wasn't nearly as disarmingly handsome as his older brother.

"Don't frown at me," Dante said lightly. "We're family and you'll soon find that the DeFiores are huggers."

"Thanks for the warning."

From what Lizzie had told her most of the family lived outside the city on a vineyard. Too bad there wouldn't be time to visit, but Jules didn't want to overstay her welcome or crowd the lovebirds. Her mission was to check out the groom, catch up with Lizzie and get wedding details— lots of details. It was never too soon to plan the perfect wedding, and Lizzie deserved no less.

"Let's go upstairs and get you settled." Lizzie started for the front door of the restaurant.

"Where exactly are we going?" Jules asked, looking around and trying to get her bearings.

Dante spoke up. "There are apartments above the restaurant. And the entrance is outside."

"Sounds good. We can get started right away on the wedding plans. We don't have time to waste." Jules grabbed for her purse. Before she could reach for her carry-on, Stefano had it in hand. She turned back and followed Lizzie out the door. "Do you have a date picked out? Say, next spring? Or summer?"

"That's what we wanted to talk to you about." There was hesitation in Lizzie's voice.

Jules's hand gripped the strap of her purse tighter. She sensed trouble. Were they calling the wedding off? They didn't seem to be fighting or anything. So what was the matter?

"Lizzie, at least let your sister get settled in before you get into it." Dante maneuvered her suitcase in through a side door and over to a waiting elevator.

"You're right. My head is just spinning at the moment." Lizzie turned to Jules. "Wait until you see the penthouse. It's amazing. I think our entire apartment would fit in the guest room alone."

Jules watched as Lizzie leaned over and placed a kiss on Dante's lips. A look came over her sister's face—a look of utter happiness and love. Suddenly the impact of what was about to happen struck Jules. The thought made her stomach plummet. How had she missed this before?

First, there'd been the eviction notice. Their New York apartment building was converting to expensive condos. That shock had been closely followed by the panicked search for affordable housing combined with trying to find a way to tell Lizzie that she'd had a change of heart about her future. All in all, she'd been pretty caught up in the drama that was her life.

But even with all of that, she couldn't hide from this piece of reality forever. The backs of her eyes stung, and she blinked repeatedly. The life she'd always known—Lizzie and Jules joined at the hip—was over.

She was now alone in this great big world.

The smiles.
The I-love-you looks.

The kisses.

Stefano couldn't wait to bolt for the door. His younger brother certainly had it bad for Lizzie. Whatever was going on with the wedding, they certainly weren't about to call it off. Maybe they'd already eloped. Stefano ground his teeth together. The thought of his brother doing something so impulsive—so reckless—had Stefano's whole body tensing up.

He knew what it was to love and lose. He knew the pain...and the guilt that ate at him. He didn't want Dante to end up like him or their widowed father. DeFiore men inevitably ended up alone—one way or the other. Dante knew all of this; he just chose to ignore it. Avoidance, it was a DeFiore trait. So was stubbornness. And he couldn't forget to toss in a driving need for independence.

"What has you so quiet this evening, big brother?" Dante clapped him on the back.

"I have a lot on my mind."

"Really? Do tell?" Dante moved through the open floor plan from the ultramodern black-and-white living room to the stainless steel galley kitchen.

"Nothing you'd be interested in hearing."

"Aka it's vineyard business." Dante pulled open the fridge and perused the contents. "Want something to drink? Looks like Lizzie stocked up on everything for her sister's arrival."

"I'm good."

Dante withdrew a bottle of water and unscrewed the top. "Okay, what's eating you?"

Before Stefano could think up something to tell his brother besides the truth, the women returned. *Thank goodness.* He could now escape before the lovey-dovey stuff started again.

"Isn't it wonderful?" Lizzie smiled. When her eyes landed on Dante, she glowed with happiness.

"It really is amazing." Jules twisted her hands together, looking a bit uncomfortable as the lovebirds radiated toward each other as if by magnetic force. "Well, don't keep us in suspense—what did you have to tell us about the wedding?"

Stefano's gaze moved from Jules, with her now sad eyes and her drawn face, to the happy couple who looked as though they belonged on the front of a Valentine's Day greeting card. With their arms draped around each other's waist, they looked lovingly into each other's eyes. Stefano glanced away. He truly wanted it to last for them, but the DeFiore statistics were against them.

"Shall we tell them everything now?" Lizzie stared adoringly up at his brother.

Stefano's gut rolled nauseously. There was only so much sugary sweetness he could stomach before he became ill. Had he and Gianna ever looked that ridiculously in love? If they had, he couldn't recall.

"Tell them," Dante prodded. "It isn't like it's a secret. And to pull this off, we're going to need their help."

The smile faded from Lizzie's face. "I guess you're right—"

"Guys, what is it?" Stefano hadn't meant to lose his patience, but he really did want to get out of there. He needed to head back to the vineyard, where he could lose himself in work and forget the lovey-dovey stuff as well as Jules's little purple butterfly that still tempted and teased.

He felt Jules's narrowed gaze on him. He ignored her as he crossed his arms, willing this to be over. Soon.

"Well, the thing is," Lizzie began, reaching for Dante's hand, "the reason we couldn't pick you up at the airport is that the studio contacted us for a teleconference."

Jules implored her sister with her big emerald eyes. "Would you just tell us what they said?"

"They want to spotlight our wedding on the show—our very own cooking show."

"That's wonderful!" Jules rushed over and hugged her sister.

Stefano held his place. His gut grew uneasy. There was more to follow. He was certain of it.

When the girls pulled apart, Lizzie continued, "The thing is we have to have the wedding in the next two months—"

"What?" Jules's eyes grew round. "That's not possible. Do they know what it takes to plan a wedding?"

"They were really excited about the idea. They said it could really boost ratings." Lizzie clutched Dante's hand. "I...I told them we could do it."

"You did what?" Jules's face filled with color as she pressed her lips together.

Stefano didn't know if Jules was going to yell or cry. And Lizzie looked upset, too. Honestly, he didn't know what the big deal was. The only thing you needed was the bride and groom, and the rest was a bunch of froufrou.

"Jules, you don't understand. This is the opportunity of a lifetime."

His gaze ping-ponged between the two women. Tempers were rising. If someone didn't do something, this happy reunion was going to end up in a fight. And he didn't want to see that happen—especially when the disagreement would be over something so stupid.

"Ladies, I'm sure it can be worked out. After all, it's only a wedding. How hard can it be?"

Suddenly everyone's attention was on him. The two women looked as though they would send poisonous arrows his way if they could. Dante smiled and shook his head, but he didn't say a word. So much for receiving any support from his own flesh and blood.

Jules marched over to him. She planted her hands on her hips and lifted her chin. "Exactly how many weddings have you planned?"

He wasn't about to get into that debate, but when he opened his mouth there was a distinct disconnect between his brain and his vocal cords. "It can't be that hard. After all, the venue is all taken care of."

"The venue is only one part of a wedding."

"So you pick out some pretty dresses and order a cake. Nothing to stress out about."

Jules glared at him and turned away. "Said like a man who has never planned a wedding."

Lizzie nodded as though in total agreement. "I know this is short notice. But Dante and I were talking, and we really don't want to wait a whole year, anyway."

Jules's brows lifted. "Is there some other news we should know?"

Color rose in Lizzie's cheeks. "No. Nothing like that. We're just anxious to get on with the rest of our lives."

"But I'm leaving in a week." Jules worried her bottom lip.

"I know. But if Dante and I buy you an air-line ticket for a later date, to make up for the one you'll be forfeiting, would you consider staying until after the wedding? Please."

Stefano's focus zeroed in on Jules. Part of

him wanted her to stick with her original plans and leave soon. But a much stronger part of him wanted a chance to check out the butterfly tattoo a little closer—

No! What was he thinking? He didn't want anything to do with her. Butterfly or no butterfly. He had no intention of getting too close—of feeling too much. The price was too steep. And on top of it all, he didn't deserve a second chance at happiness.

"Yes, I'll stay." Jules crossed her arms and gave Lizzie a firm look. "You know that this is the craziest thing we've ever done. Whoever heard of putting together a wedding in two months?"

"We can do it." Lizzie looked over at Dante. "Didn't I tell you she's amazing?"

"Yes, you did."

Dante swept Lizzie into his arms and kissed her like there was no tomorrow. Stefano averted his gaze and ended up staring at Jules. She looked just as uncomfortable as he felt. No one should be as much in love as them. Thankfully he was leaving.

At the DeFiore Vineyard there were no couples in love—no uncomfortable moments. Only memories of mistakes that couldn't be undone.

CHAPTER THREE

WAS THAT WHAT it was like to be hooked on someone?

Jules gave a slight shake of her head. She wouldn't know. She'd never let herself get that close to anyone. She glanced at the engaged couple, who were gazing longingly into each other's eyes. It was as though they had forgotten that anyone else was in the room. She considered making a joking comment, but she couldn't bring herself to do it. She'd never seen Lizzie so happy...ever. And she didn't want to do anything to ruin it.

"I should be going." Stefano hedged his way toward the door.

"Wait." Jules sent him a desperate look. He couldn't just leave her there. "Could you give me a ride?"

She may not want to ruin Lizzie's happiness, but that didn't mean she wanted to be subjected to it in large quantities. No way was Stefano escaping this den of love and leaving her trapped.

There was only so much she could take of this sugary sweetness. And her teeth already ached.

Lizzie pulled away from Dante. "A ride where?"

"To get a hotel room."

"Why would you do that?" V-shaped lines formed between Lizzie's brows. "After all, this will be your home during school breaks."

"What?" This was news to her.

Before Jules could find the words to set her sister straight, Stefano stepped forward. "Jules might enjoy staying at the villa. It's quite spacious, and it'll be helpful for her to see where the wedding will take place."

Lizzie's mouth opened, but nothing came out. Jules had the feeling she was wearing a similar expression. The man who didn't approve of her appearance and who thought weddings were a waste of time was now suggesting she stay with him? She wasn't so sure how she felt about his offer.

Lizzie's gaze narrowed as it darted between Jules and Stefano. "Thank you, Stefano. But I'm sure Jules will be more comfortable staying here."

Jules swallowed and straightened her shoulders. "I think a hotel would be best."

"You really don't want to stay here?" Lizzie's voice grew soft, eroding Jules's resolve.

Dante stepped up and pulled Lizzie close. Her

head tilted against his shoulder as if they'd been leaning on each other for years.

Dante met Jules's gaze. "You are welcome here. Anytime. For as long as you want. It's your home now, too."

"Thank you." It really meant a lot coming from him, but it still didn't change her mind. She couldn't impose on them. But she didn't have the money to stay in a hotel indefinitely. She turned to Stefano. "How far is the vineyard from here?"

"It's a bit of a drive."

"But my brother will be happy to get you back and forth." Dante smiled as though he really liked the idea.

Jules worried her bottom lip. It was only logical that she go home with Stefano, and he seemed fine with the idea. So why was she throwing up roadblocks?

"I guess Stefano's right. With the wedding being pushed up, we need to get started right away." And then Jules got an idea and turned to her foster sister. "Maybe you should come with me."

Lizzie's expression filled with worry. "I'd really like to, but I have to stay here as they want to start filming this week. I'm sorry."

"Oh. I see." It was going to be challenging planning a wedding without the bride constantly on hand, but somehow they'd make it work.

"But I do have some notes." Lizzie rushed back the hallway and soon returned with a notebook. She handed it over. "I wrote out a bunch of ideas and attached pictures I cut out from magazines. How about you look over these and then we'll talk?"

"Sounds good. But what about your dress? Will you be able to get something in such a short time frame?"

Lizzie sent her a knowing smile. "I had the same worry. I ran out as soon as the studio proposed the idea, and I found exactly what I wanted. It's being altered right now."

"Great." Check the most important item off the list. "Did you happen to find one for me?"

"Actually I found three that will work. All you have to do is try them on and see which looks the best."

Okay, so maybe this rushed wedding wasn't going to be as horrible to plan as she'd initially envisioned. It wasn't like Lizzie would turn into bridezilla or anything. Her foster sister had never been a prima donna.

"Are you sure you won't stay here?" Lizzie begged her with both word and look. "I was really hoping we could catch up on everything and watch some old movies together."

If it were only Lizzie in the apartment, she wouldn't hesitate to stay. But even now she noticed how Dante and Lizzie gravitated together. They couldn't keep their hands off each other. And if she were perfectly honest, she wanted to see the vineyard. From everything she'd heard, it was gorgeous. Who would pass up a chance to stay at an Italian villa?

Once you got past his solemn attitude, her host wasn't too bad, either. She glanced over at Stefano, who was talking with his brother. Okay, so he was a lot more like droolworthy. Her stomach fluttered. Thankfully the attraction was a one-way avenue. He'd already made it perfectly clear that she wasn't his type.

She glanced away—but not soon enough. Lizzie raised her eyebrows, followed by a questioning look. Jules rolled her eyes and shook her head. The last thing she needed was Lizzie thinking that she had a thing for Stefano. He was much too serious for her. And she didn't have time for a guy. She had other things on her mind—like planning a rushed wedding and figuring out what to do with her future once she withdrew from grad school.

"How are things coming with school?" Lizzie stepped closer to her.

"Uh…good." That was strange. It was as if Lizzie could read her mind. She considered telling Lizzie her decision and getting it over with, but not with the guys in the room. This delicate conversation was going to require some uninterrupted privacy.

"Are you ready to go?" Stefano sent her a direct look that said he wanted to escape honeymoon central.

"Yes, I am. Just let me grab my bag."

"I've got it." Stefano gripped the handle.

Jules turned back to Lizzie, who had an expectant look on her face. "We'll talk later. I'm so happy for you. And don't worry about a thing. I promise we'll plan the best wedding. Ever."

Lizzie's worried expression eased. "Thank you. You're the best."

"I'll remember that you said that." Jules smiled, so happy to see her sister again. "We have a lot of work ahead of us."

What in the world had he been thinking?

Stefano shook his head. Obviously he hadn't been thinking, at least not clearly. What he knew about playing host wouldn't even fill up his mother's thimble—a memento that his father kept on his dresser. And what Stefano knew about making women happy was practically nonexistent. His wife could attest to that—if she were still alive. Guilt weighed heavy on his shoulders.

It was just one more reason that taking Jules home with him wasn't a good idea. Because once you got past all the makeup and distinctive clothes, there was something special about Jules—something that intrigued him. And that was definitely not a good thing.

But he couldn't just leave her stranded there with those two. His brother could barely keep his hands off Lizzie. Not that he could blame him.

But there was no way anyone could convince Stefano to stay in that apartment—no matter how spacious it was. There was only so much of that mushy stuff that one could handle. Regardless of his hesitation, Jules didn't deserve to play the third wheel.

"Thank you."

Her voice startled him out of his thoughts. "What?"

"Thank you for helping me out back there. I don't think I could have stood to watch them much longer. Did you ever see such a happy couple?"

He shook his head. At last, they had something in common. "They certainly have it bad for each other."

"You noticed that, too?"

He nodded, keeping his eyes on the road. "What do you think about their rush to say *I do*?"

"I was beginning to think that Lizzie was never going to settle down with a family of her own, especially after—well, anyway, it's full steam ahead."

After what? He wanted to ask, but he didn't. He just hoped that Dante knew what Jules was referring to. He wasn't crazy about the rushed engagement and even less so about the hurried wedding. He wished Dante would take his time and give the whole marriage idea more thought.

Perhaps now Stefano wasn't the only one with reservations. He'd noticed the brief frown that had crossed Jules's face back at the love nest when she thought no one was looking. Maybe she'd had a change of heart about this whirlwind romance.

Could it be he had an ally—someone who thought the happy couple should slow down and see reason? Sure, the television people were anxious for the wedding. The only thing that mattered to them was their ratings. But marriage was about so much more than a popularity contest. It was a lifelong commitment—one that could have devastating consequences if you weren't careful.

He cleared his throat. "That sure was a surprise about them pushing the wedding up so far. It's only a matter of weeks away. I wonder if they're doing the right thing."

He took his focus off the road for a moment and glanced over to find Jules studying him suspiciously. Definitely not a good sign. It would seem that he'd read her reactions all wrong.

"What are you worried about?" she asked. "Don't you like Lizzie? Don't you think she's good enough for your brother?"

"Whoa! Slow down. That isn't what I meant." Why in the world had he even opened his mouth? He should have just left well enough alone.

He kept glancing between Jules and the road. She crossed her arms and arched a brow at him. She was waiting for an explanation, and he didn't know exactly what to say. He didn't want to open his mouth and insert his freshly polished dress shoe. But she didn't look as though she was about to let him off the proverbial hook anytime soon.

He sighed. "What I meant was that if it's real between them, there's no need to rush—no matter what the television studio says. They can take their time—"

"That's not the real truth, is it?" When he didn't have an immediate denial, Jules barreled on. "The truth is you know about Lizzie's past and you don't think that she's good enough to marry into the DeFiore family."

"That's not true." He wished that was the case. If his disapproval was the only obstacle Dante and Lizzie had to face, their future would be paved in rose petals. But the truth was he thought they made a great couple—a couple totally in love with each other. The problem with love was that it was blind and deaf to the truth. And sooner or later, devastation would plan a sneak attack—it always did. But how did he explain any of that to Jules? Unless you had lived through it—twice in his case—you just couldn't truly understand.

Marriage to a DeFiore ended with dire consequences.

"Then what is it?" Jules continued to stare at him. "Why are you against this wedding?"

"I'm not. At least not as far as them being together."

"But…"

He couldn't do it.

Telling Jules the whole truth wasn't an option. He couldn't pry open that door to his past—to relive the pain. And though he barely knew her, he couldn't stand the thought of Jules turning those luminous green eyes on him in judgment, followed by condemnation. Gianna's family still looked at him that way. He'd finally accepted that they'd always blame him.

Pain and worry drowned out his common sense, and he spoke from his tattered heart. "I don't think they know each other well enough yet. Heck, even when you've known someone for years, there's still so much adjustment you have to make."

"You sound as though you know this first-hand."

He shrugged off her comment.

There he'd gone and done it. He'd cracked open the door to his past. And now he just hoped he could get it closed again before too many memories leaked out. The painful image of his wife's mangled car being towed away had him gripping the steering wheel tighter.

He choked down the jagged lump in his throat. "The point is that I like Lizzie. I think she's great."

"You do?" There was a note of surprise mingled with happiness in Jules's voice. "Really?"

He nodded and then switched on the turn signal as they neared the entrance to the vineyard. "I just don't want them to rush things and then find out later that they made a mistake."

"Is that what you think they're doing? Making a mistake?"

He shrugged again. "I think love is a two-edged sword. And if you aren't careful, you'll get cut."

He didn't look at her this time, but he could feel her steady gaze on him. He wasn't going any further with this conversation. He didn't owe her any other explanations. None whatsoever.

CHAPTER FOUR

HONESTY RANG OUT in Stefano's voice.

But could Jules believe her ears?

Did he truly like her sister? Or was he just telling her what he thought she wanted to hear? Jules wanted to believe him. Truly she did. But there was something more to his hesitation than the wedding being bumped up. And that made her intensely curious.

"Here we are." Stefano's deep voice with its heavy accent drew her out of her thoughts.

With the setting sun at her back, Jules stared out over the vast sloping green fields. It was the most gorgeous evening she'd ever seen. Brilliant pinks and purples painted the sky, while the symmetrical rows of bountiful grapevines were shadowed against the horizon. It was a little piece of heaven on earth.

"You live here?"

"The DeFiore family has lived here for generations."

He turned the car down a small lane. Off to

the side sat a painted wooden sign. Gold letters on a deep purple background spelled out DeFiore Winery. It was very stylish. Something told her this villa was going to be more impressive than she'd been imagining. Already the landscape had an essence of romance and blissful happiness written all over it.

What exactly had she gotten herself into by agreeing to stay here?

A sexy Italian by her side, the poshest car she'd ever ridden in and the most magnificent countryside added up to trouble. She was certain of it.

Then again, why fight it? Why not enjoy it? This was her treat for working so hard to graduate with high honors from college. Granted she'd been a couple of years older than her classmates, a result of enrolling late because of a financial hardship. But none of that meant the classes had been any easier for her.

"Here we are." Stefano slowed the car to a stop outside a sprawling villa. "I hope you'll be comfortable here."

"I…I'm certain I will be."

She gazed up at the sprawling three-story villa. This was more like a colorful mansion than a cozy country home. She caught herself gaping and pressed her lips together. Bright blue shutters adorned each window and door. The color contrasted well with the sunny yellow walls and the red tile roof. Someone sure appreciated vibrant colors. And she couldn't blame them. It made a happy, welcoming statement.

The various balconies beckoned to her. Was it possible that her room would have one? She hoped so. She envisioned strolling out there to enjoy her morning coffee. *Wow*. People really lived like this?

She couldn't help but glance around looking for someone with a video camera. But there was no one in sight. Somehow it was hard to imagine that this villa was someone's home and not a prop on a television show about the rich and famous. And Stefano could easily fit the part of a sexy movie star who set women's heart's racing—except hers. She was immune to his charms.

Stefano opened the car door for her, and she stepped out. "This place is amazing."

"Thank you."

"It'll be the perfect backdrop for the wedding." She glanced around, searching for the ideal spot for Lizzie and Dante to say their vows.

"You're thinking of having the ceremony outside?"

A gentle breeze tickled her skin. "Of course. With such a beautiful setting, it's not even worth considering any other place."

"If you don't mind me asking, what do you know about planning a wedding? Are you—I mean, have you been married?"

She laughed. She couldn't help it. The thought of her making such a commitment was akin to asking her if she could sprout wings and fly. Sure, she hoped that Lizzie would live happily ever after, but, as for herself, she didn't believe in putting her future in someone else's hands.

"I'm a confirmed bachelorette."

His dark brows lifted. "Really?"

"Don't look so shocked. Men don't have the market cornered on staying single."

He rubbed the back of his neck. "I guess I just never met a woman that didn't believe in roses, platitudes and promises of forever."

"Well, now you have."

"So I have."

Though she'd never admit it, standing here in this little piece of heaven on earth with a man whose thoughts extended beyond his zipper, she could at last understand why some women went the romantic forever route. She turned, and their gazes connected. She should glance away, but she didn't want to. Not yet. Her stomach quivered. She'd never experienced such a sensation around a man. What was it about him that had her body betraying her?

Whatever it was, she'd have to be careful around him. No way was she going to fall for some unrealistic fantasy. She knew for a fact that the people you were supposed to trust the most were the first to let you down—the first to inflict pain. Her fa-

ther had done it first. And then her mother had let
her down in the worst way.

Jules refused to let herself get close enough to
a man for him to hurt her.

The following morning, Stefano found himself
lingering in the updated kitchen longer than necessary. Instead of his normal one cup of *caffè*,
he'd just finished his second when he turned to
refill his cup and found the pot empty.

Oh, this was ridiculous. He was stalling, and by
the look on Maria's face, their cook/housekeeper
knew it, too. Thankfully she didn't say a word
about his beautiful houseguest. Maria turned her
back to him and set about making a fresh pot.

He carried his empty cup to the sink.

Maria tilted her head to look at him. "If you
wait, you can have more *caffè*."

"No, thanks." He forced a smile before gazing
out the window at the brilliant morning sunshine
casting a golden glow over the ordered rows of
grapevines. "I'm just tired today. I was up late
last night catching up on some paperwork for the
winery. Harvest time will be here soon. We need
to be prepared."

Maria's dark head nodded before she moved to
the fridge. *Just great.* Now he was talking like a
blathering fool. He shouldn't be standing around—

waiting for Jules. She'd be fine on her own. He'd shown her all around the villa yesterday.

The less he thought about the woman who wore far too much makeup, the better. His work was waiting for him, and it wasn't getting done standing here.

"Thanks for breakfast."

"Don't worry so much. Everything will work out."

Before he could ask what she meant, he heard footsteps. He turned to find Jules standing there in black shorts and a sheer long-sleeved black top. But what sent his heart slamming into his ribs was the black bra that was visible beneath her top. Wait. It was more than a bra, but not much more. There was a strip of stomach visible, and the spaghetti straps left her arms bare beneath the sheer top.

His first instinct was to get her one of his long-sleeved shirts to put on. What if one of the workmen saw her like this? His gut knotted up. Then again, why should he care what clothes she wore? Or who looked at her? But he couldn't shrug off the unsettling feeling of protectiveness. He didn't want other men ogling her.

The thought brought him up short. He couldn't be jealous. That was ridiculous. He had no claim on her. Nor would he. She could traipse around in her birthday suit and it'd mean nothing to him.

So then why was the sight of her in that sexy

little outfit warming his blood? His jaw tightened, and his body tensed. It'd be best if he thought of something else—and quick.

"Good morning." She smiled as though she didn't have a care in the world. "I didn't mean to sleep in so late. I guess all of the traveling is catching up with me."

Stefano's mouth went dry, and his mind went blank. He should say something. Yet his tongue stuck to the roof of his mouth. He was staring. And he couldn't tear his gaze from her.

Maria stepped between them and offered Jules breakfast—a hearty one. As Jules dug in, the fact that the slip of a woman had such a hearty appetite didn't escape his attention. When her eyes met his there was a twinkle of amusement in them.

He swallowed past the lump in his throat. "Did you sleep well?"

"I did. I opened the window and a cool breeze put me straight to sleep."

He sure hadn't slept well—not at all. Thoughts of the little butterfly tattoo had fluttered through his mind. His attention strayed to her chest, but the material obscured his view. Just as well. He was better off not thinking of it at all.

Work. Concentrate on today's tasks.

"I'm heading out to the fields."

Jules's eyes lit up. "Are you going to pick grapes? It looks like such fun on television."

He chuckled. It was refreshing having someone around who didn't think she was an expert when it came to the vines. "No. It's not that time of the year. But at harvest time, you're welcome to come back and join us."

"Thanks." The enthusiasm in her voice made him smile. "I just might take you up on the offer. But is it hard to learn?"

"No. Anyone can do it. I'm sure you'll take right to it."

Her lips pursed together. "I'll definitely keep it in mind. Thank you for the invite."

He mentally kicked himself for extending such a ridiculous invitation. Like she was going to fly all the way back to Italy to pick grapes. Yeah, right. But what if she did? Hope ballooned in his chest, and he immediately squelched it.

"If you aren't picking grapes, what do you do?"

"There's always something that needs tending. Right now, I'm going to thin the shoots."

"Interesting." Her brows scrunched together. "Sorry. I don't know much about making wine. Actually I don't know anything at all about it except how to drink it."

It was on the tip of his tongue to offer to show her the basics, but spending time with her wasn't a good idea. Besides, she was only feigning interest in the grapes to be nice. After all, why would this city girl be interested in a bunch of plants?

He assured himself that she had plenty of wedding stuff to keep her occupied.

His grandfather shuffled into the kitchen using a walker to assist him. Ever since Nonno had a stroke, forcing him to hand over the reins of Ristorante Massimo to Dante, he'd been living at the villa. Nonno was his mother's father and the only grandfather Stefano had even known. He loved him dearly and was so relieved to find that Nonno was starting to pull himself out of that dark place he'd briefly visited after being forced into retirement.

Stefano spoke up. "Nonno, this is Jules, Lizzie's sister. She got in last night. Jules, this is my grandfather, Massimo."

"I'm old, not deaf." His grandfather frowned at him before turning a lopsided smile to Jules. "Welcome."

Stefano smiled and shook his head. His grandfather still had an eye for women. Some things didn't change. Stefano watched as his grandfather interacted with Jules. The frown lines on his face eased, and that took years off his appearance. Obviously Stefano wasn't the only one to find a special quality in Jules that made the world a brighter place.

Jules smiled brightly at Nonno. "Lizzie has told me a lot about you, too."

"All good, I hope." His grandfather's speech

was still a bit slurred, but Stefano was either getting used to it or his grandfather's therapy was helping him.

"Only the best. She told me you are quite handsome and a wonderful conversationalist."

Nonno joined Jules at the table. He reached out and squeezed her hand. Her smile lit up her eyes. Jealousy poked at Stefano. She never smiled that brightly at him. She always remained reserved, as if she were prepared for him to bite her at any moment. And now that his grandfather was there it was as though she'd forgotten he was even in the room.

"Well, I'll let you eat your breakfast." Stefano needed to get away—to get some fresh air to clear his thoughts.

His grandfather didn't say a word as he sipped at his *caffè*.

At last, Jules turned to Stefano as though she'd just remembered his presence. "I shouldn't have slept so late. Lizzie will be here at lunch so that we can get started with the wedding plans."

"Then I'll leave you to your planning." He slipped out the door feeling torn between the relief of escaping and the disappointment that he wouldn't see her again until dinner.

CHAPTER FIVE

"I WAS BEGINNING to think that I'd never find you." Jules strode up to Stefano. She'd just about given up when she spotted him checking the vines.

He furrowed his brow. "I thought you'd be inside making wedding plans with Lizzie."

"She canceled it."

"The wedding—"

"No. It's still on." Heat rushed up and filled Jules's face. "I meant she canceled our plans for today. She said that she had to stick around the restaurant for a video conference with the people at the studio. Something about finalizing some details for next week's taping. They sure have a lot of meetings for a reality show."

Stefano stepped away from the grapevines and joined Jules in the rutted dirt path. "That show seems to take up more and more of their time. When my brother started coming home less and less on the weekends, he blamed it on filming conflicts. Me, personally, I thought it was because he wanted alone time with Lizzie, but it seems now he's been telling the truth."

"That's too bad. But at least they're happy. And I suppose it won't last forever. This is their fifteen minutes of fame."

He dusted his hands off on his faded jeans. "I was just heading back to the barn."

"The barn?"

He pointed to a large building off in the distance with a stone facade. "It's where we produce the wine. Beneath it is the barrel cellar."

"Do you mind if I tag along? There's something I want to ask you." Since Lizzie couldn't drive out to the vineyard, she'd asked if Jules would mind meeting them in Rome the next day. It sounded important, but Lizzie had been very closemouthed and said they'd talk at dinner.

"Sure. Come on." They fell in step, side by side. "What's on your mind?"

The thought of begging him for a ride into the city didn't sit well with her. She didn't like relying on others. Lizzie had said to bring Stefano along, but with all the work he had to do, would he want to drive all that way just to have dinner? She decided to put off asking him. She was enjoying his good mood, and this was her chance to get to know him a little better.

"It's big." She pointed to the wine barn. "Really big."

"It wasn't always that size. My father and I have done a lot to expand the business. Although we made a point of keeping the outside looking traditional, the inside has been totally modernized. We want to grow DeFiore winery into a household name. Hopefully it can be passed on from generation to generation."

"I'm sure your children will appreciate all of your efforts—"

"I don't have kids." His quick response caught her off guard.

"I kinda guessed that. But you will as soon as you meet the right woman. Isn't that what all of this is for?"

"No." He rubbed the back of his neck. "Maybe Dante's kids will take an interest in the business."

Jules glanced over at him, noticing the strained look on his face as he kept his line of vision straight ahead. She wondered about his strong reaction to the thought of having kids.

Maybe it had something to do with her surprise in finding that she was the only woman aside from Maria living at the villa. Where were the women? Stefano was very handsome. In fact, if she were looking for fun beneath the Italian sun, he'd be first on her list. Was he still mourning his wife? Not that it was any of her business. But still she was curious.

"How about you?" Stefano's voice drew her out of her thoughts.

"What?"

"Are you interested in having a family?"

He was the first person to ask her that question. Not even Lizzie had asked her. And she supposed she owed him some sort of answer since she'd brought up the subject in the first place.

"Do I look like mother material?"

"Sure. I guess."

"You aren't even looking at me."

He stopped walking and turned to her. Silence ensued as he stared at her. "I think that beneath all of that makeup lies a beautiful woman who can have whatever she sets her mind on."

Her heart stopped. He thought she was beautiful? This was yet another thing that no one had ever said to her. What did she say now?

She moved her tongue from where it was stuck to the top of her mouth, hoping her voice would work. "Thanks. But you don't have to say that just to make me feel better."

"I'm not." His eyes darkened as he continued to stare at her as though he was truly seeing her. "There's something special about you."

A fluttering sensation filled her chest, and all she could think about was sinking into his arms and finding out if his kisses were as romantic as the ones she watched in the black-and-white movies that played late at night when she was alone while her friends were out on dates.

"I'm out of the loop on what's in style as far as women's fashions. I suppose that the makeup and dark clothes are a fashion statement."

Jules glanced down at her black-on-black ensemble. She never really stopped to think about her appearance. She'd been dressing like this for so many years that it was just natural for her. It hid the ugly scars that lurked beneath—a reminder of a part of her life that was best left hidden and buried.

"Actually, it's just my style."

"I see. It…it's different from how the women in these parts dress. In the village, things are more simplistic than you'll find in Rome or Milan."

Normally she'd have taken that as an insult, but he'd already said he thought she was beautiful… beneath the makeup. So maybe he was just stating a fact. She stood out around here. But she didn't have anything else to wear—anything that would make her fit in better. Not that she planned to—fit in, that is.

She toyed with a loose thread on the hem of her top. "It's just so different back in New York. It's like a melting pot of styles and trends."

"I can imagine. But I'm confused. What does your appearance have to do with you becoming a mother?"

Back to that subject—the one she didn't want to delve into. "I'm not having kids."

"As in ever?"

"As in never ever. I wouldn't have a clue how to be a good mother." And there she'd gone and blurted out more than she'd intended to say—more than she normally shared with anyone.

Stefano started walking again toward the barn, and she fell in step beside him, waiting and wondering what he'd ask next. They moved along quietly for a few minutes. A gentle breeze brushed over Jules's face and made her pigtails flutter. But it was the man to her left that had her chest all aquiver. He really thought she was beautiful? Her heart tumbled.

As they neared the large stone structure, Stefano cleared his throat. "You'd be surprised at what people are capable of when their hearts are involved."

She shook her head. "Trust me. I didn't have a good role model."

"I'm sorry to hear that."

Not as sorry as I am.

Just then she heard something. A squeak? A squeal? A cry?

She stopped walking. "Did you hear that?"

Stefano stopped and glanced back at her. "I don't hear anything. What is it—"

"Shhh…" Her gaze darted around the foundation of the building, where the grass was higher.

If it was a rat, she was going to scream and jump on Stefano's back. She may be pushing to gain her independence from her foster sister, but that didn't mean she didn't have a weakness or two. And rodents gave her the willies. Still curiosity drove her on.

Squeak.

"Did you hear it that time?"

He nodded. "I wouldn't worry about it. I'm sure it's just some sort of wildlife that can take care of itself. Come on. I'll give you the unofficial tour of the winery."

"We can't leave. Not yet. What if it's hurt?"

Stefano arched a brow. "Didn't you just get done telling me that you weren't the motherly type?"

"I'm not." Though deep down she wished someday she could be the kind of mother that she'd dreamed of. "But that doesn't mean that I'm heartless. The creature might be starved or worse."

She didn't want to think about the worse part. She'd always had a tender spot for animals, even though she'd never been able to have a pet. Her foster homes wouldn't allow animals. And then the apartment lease forbade them. But now that she was moving, perhaps she'd look for a pet-friendly apartment.

She hunched over and started searching around the shrubs and through the greenery along the side of the building. When she glanced over her shoulder, she found Stefano standing there staring at her.

"Don't just stand there. Help me." She didn't wait for his response as she turned and continued her hunt.

There was a distinct sigh from Stefano followed by the sound of his approaching footsteps. She wished whatever it was would squeak again. She couldn't see any signs of life. What was it? And where was it?

"Is this what you're searching for?"

Jules immediately straightened and turned. Her gaze landed on a fuzzy ball of orange fur. "What is it?"

Stefano chuckled. "Don't you city girls know a kitten when you see one?"

"A kitten?" Her mouth fell open, and she forced it shut. She moved closer. "Is it yours?"

He shook his head. "Not mine."

"Then how did it get here?" She glanced around, not seeing any nearby houses.

"Sometimes when people don't want animals, they drop them off. I don't know why they think this is a good place to leave animals, especially cats. It isn't like we're a dairy farm or anything."

She stuck out her hand to pet it, then paused just inches from the ball of fluff. "Is...is it okay?"

"I'm no vet but..." He lifted the little thing up and gave it a once-over. "I think it's scared to death and starved. Otherwise, I think it's okay."

Jules blew out a breath she hadn't known she'd been holding. "Can I pet it?"

His brow crinkled. "Sure. It isn't that fragile."

Her fingertips stroked the dirty and tangled fur. She could feel its little ribs as they moved in and out with each breath. And then it turned to look at her. Its crusty little blue eyes peered at her. In that moment, Jules's heart melted. How could anyone dump such a sweet little thing?

"Do you want to hold it?" Stefano held out the kitten to her.

"Sure. But...but I don't want to hurt it."

"Trust me—you'll be fine."

She held out her hands, and then there was a little pile of fur in them. She didn't know that anything could be so featherlight. Her fingers instinctively stroked the fur. She could so relate to this kitten. She knew what it was like to be abused by those who are supposed to care for you.

"Aww...it's so sweet." She lifted the kitten until they were face-to-face. "Don't worry. You're safe now."

As she started back toward the house, Stefano called out to her, "What about the tour of the winery?"

"It'll have to wait. Apricot needs some food."

"Apricot?" There was a pause and then the sound of him catching up to her. "What are you planning to do with…Apricot?"

"Feed her, of course." What did he think she was going to do with the poor little thing?

"I meant after that. Do you really think it's such a good idea to name it?"

She saw the concern in his eyes. What was he worried about? That she didn't have a clue what she was doing? That somehow she'd hurt Apricot? Maybe he was right. She didn't know what she was doing, but she was willing to learn.

"We can't keep calling her 'it.' That's not a name. And I may not know anything about cats, but I can learn. That's what the internet is for." And then a worrisome thought formed. "Or are you worried about having the cat in the house?"

"The cat in the house is fine. It's a big place, and if you keep it in your suite of rooms, no one will even know it's there."

As they walked on in silence, Jules's nerves kicked up. She really didn't know what she was doing. What if she did hurt the kitten? After all, she'd never taken care of anyone but herself, and even then Lizzie had always been around.

This is why she wasn't having children—ever. She didn't know thing one about taking care of others. And judging by the worried expression on Stefano's face, he agreed. She glanced down at Apricot. Someone had to do his or her best for the kitten. And for the moment that was her.

"What did you want to talk to me about, you know, before the whole cat thing?"

That's right. She still had to spring the idea of a trip into the city on him. "What exactly are you doing tomorrow?"

CHAPTER SIX

WHY EXACTLY HAD he agreed to dinner out?

Stefano sat stiffly in a chair in one of Rome's finest hotels. Jules and Lizzie were chatting non-stop about wedding preparations. And he wanted to be anywhere but listening to things like guest lists, linen choices and table settings. All it did was stir up long-forgotten memories.

His wedding to Gianna had started with such promise. Then the problems had set in—inconsequential things at first. A comment about a forgotten toothpaste cap seemed so minor. Then things escalated to a litany of how he'd lost interest in her. He'd thought it was what every married couple went through as they adjusted to married life.

He tried to do better. He started taking Gianna to Rome as often as his work would allow him to be away. She'd always loved the city. And he'd loved spoiling her. But when he'd mentioned starting a family, she'd gotten angry. She didn't want to be trapped at the vineyard with a baby. She wasn't ready to settle down into family life. She wanted the money the vineyard provided, but she didn't want anything to do with a quiet country life. Stefano tried, but he just couldn't understand why she didn't want a family of their own. Wasn't that just a natural progression of marriage—having babies?

"Hey, man, what has you so quiet?" Dante leaned back in his chair after the server removed the now empty dishes from the table.

"Nothing." He shrugged off the unwanted memories.

"Don't tell me that. I know you. And something is eating at you."

It was true. His brother could still read him quite well. He'd really been there for him after Gianna's death. And the fact that Dante had witnessed what he'd gone through after losing Gianna either made Dante brave for going ahead with this wedding or foolish. Stefano wasn't sure which was the case.

"Are you really serious about wanting to move the wedding to this hotel?" Stefano wanted to turn the conversation away from himself. "I thought you wanted to get married at the vineyard. What changed?"

Dante raked his fingers through his hair. "The

television people. They're making it nearly impossible to do what we want with the wedding."

"Then quit the show." Stefano never did understand why his brother was so anxious to turn his life upside down for a television show.

Dante shook his head. "I can't do that. We have a contract."

"I'm confused. What does the show have to do with your wedding?"

"A lot." Lizzie spoke up. All eyes turned to her. "That's why we asked you guys to dinner. We had a long meeting with the executives, and they need us to step up our filming."

"But why move the wedding here?" Jules echoed Stefano's question.

Lizzie fingered the edge of the white linen napkin. "Because the time I have available to plan the wedding is very limited. I don't know how often we'll be able to get out to the vineyard before the big day. So if we have the wedding here in Rome, it'll be more convenient."

"But will it be what you truly want? After all, it's your big day—the biggest of your life. Shouldn't it be what you want and not what's easiest?" Jules sent her foster sister a determined look.

Stefano didn't think this wedding was such a great idea, but he had to agree with Jules. If it was going to take place, it should be what they wanted and not just what was most convenient.

"Jules is right." Stefano could feel her wide-eyed stare, but he kept his vision on Lizzie before turning to Dante. "I don't hear you saying anything."

"I'm fine with whatever Lizzie decides. I want this wedding to be everything she ever dreamed it would be, whether it's here or at the vineyard."

"Thank you." Lizzie squeezed Dante's hand and gazed lovingly into his eyes. Then she turned to Jules and Stefano. "You're right—you're both right. The vineyard would be ideal. But—"

"No buts." Jules crossed her arms. "We'll make it work."

Stefano shifted in his seat. Who was this "we" that she referred to? He didn't say anything as he waited to find out exactly what she had in mind.

Lizzie peered at her sister. "I couldn't ask you to do more than you're already doing."

"You aren't asking. I'm offering."

Stefano was starting to like the sound of this. If Jules was off planning a wedding, she'd be out of his way, and maybe then he wouldn't think about those short skirts, the knee-high black boots or that little butterfly, whose purple wings at this very moment were peeping out over the plunging neckline of Jules's purple top.

"And my brother will be around to drive you

back and forth to the city. And whatever other help you'll need." Dante clapped him on the back and grinned at him as if he'd just caught him in a trap.

Stefano choked. How dare his brother automatically assume he'd be willing to continue his role as chauffeur. With all eyes on him, Stefano struggled for a neutral tone. "I have a business to run."

"Papa will help out. After all, it isn't harvest season. There shouldn't be anything too pressing."

Jules turned to him. Her eyes pleaded with him. And his resolve began to crack. Would it really be so bad? One or two trips to the city. Maybe three at most. It wasn't like he'd be doing anything but driving Jules around. How hard could that be?

"I'd really appreciate your help." Jules's lips lifted at the corners, brightening the softly lit dining room.

And in that moment, the last of his resolve shattered.

"Just let me know what you need me to do." Had he really just spoken those words?

Jules reached over and squeezed his hand. "I will. There shouldn't be too much."

Her smile reached her eyes and made them sparkle like gems. His chest filled with a funny sensation. Must be indigestion. No way was he falling for Jules. Of that he was certain.

What was up now?

Jules followed Lizzie to one of the hotel's terraces with a marble statue and a beautiful view of the city. With no other people around, they could talk openly for the first time since she'd arrived in Italy. But what did her sister want to talk about privately?

"Lizzie, what's going on?"

Her sister moved to the stone rail and stared out at the lights of Rome. They twinkled like rare jewels. But there was something more pressing on Jules's mind—Lizzie. The longer her sister remained quiet, the more worried Jules became.

At last, Lizzie turned to her. "I just want you to know that nothing between us is going to change—"

"What? Of course they're going to change. They have to." Jules took a deep breath. It was time for a healthy dose of reality. "It's time we both make lives of our own. Yours is here in Italy. Mine…well, I'm not sure where mine will be—"

"Yes, you do. Your future is in New York, getting your master's degree. Have I told you lately how proud I am of you?" Without waiting for a response, Lizzie continued, "I've been telling everyone who would listen what a smart sister I have. I even mentioned it on an upcoming television segment."

"You didn't?" Jules's stomach sank. Now the whole world would know when she dropped out. They'd all realize she was a failure.

Lizzie smiled and nodded. "I want everyone to know how proud I am of you."

Jules knew she should tell Lizzie the truth right now, but as she looked into her sister's eyes, her courage failed her. She just couldn't formulate the words to tell Lizzie that she was never going to live up to those dreams. Everything was different now. She wasn't the same girl with thoughts of changing the world.

"Don't look so sad." Lizzie squeezed her hand. "We'll stay in close contact. We can get an international phone plan." She smiled as though she'd just discovered the solution to world peace. "And we can text, email, chat on social media. It'll be just like nothing changed."

Jules pressed her lips firmly together as she sent her sister an I-don't-believe-you look. Change was the only way either of them was going to be able to truly be happy. It was scary; that was for sure. But big changes always were unsettling. Right at this moment, Jules had to be the strong one.

"The truth is—" Lizzie's eyes glistened with unshed tears "—I don't know if I can do this."

"Are you getting cold feet?" Whatever the problem was, they'd deal with it together, just like they'd been doing most of their lives.

Lizzie shook her head. "I love Dante. I love him more than I ever thought was possible."

"Then what is it?"

"It…it's you and me." Lizzie sniffled. "It's always been us against the world, and now I'm destroying that. I feel like I'm abandoning you."

Jules gave her what she hoped was a reassuring hug and then pulled back. "Our family isn't breaking up. It's expanding. I'm excited to be gaining a brother. You know I've never had one of those, and I think it's about time I did."

Lizzie sniffled again. "You're really happy about this? You aren't just saying that to make me feel better?"

Jules's finger crossed over her heart. "I swear."

Lizzie dried her eyes and smiled. "Thanks. Now what's this about you taking in a kitten?"

Stefano had mentioned it at dinner, and she'd known by the look on Lizzie's face that it had piqued her curiosity. "Apricot is adorable." Except when she tried to steal her pillow at night. "I can't wait for you to meet her. You're going to love her."

Lizzie's forehead wrinkled. "I didn't even know you wanted a cat."

The truth was she'd always loved cats, but with

getting bounced around from home to home p̶
were out of the question—unless they were the
plush stuffed ones. She was certain she'd mentioned wanting a cat in the past, but she hadn't
gone on and on about something that couldn't be.
What would be the point?

Jules shrugged. "I guess I'm full of surprises."

"I guess we both are. Who'd have ever dreamed
I'd be getting married and moving to Rome?"
Lizzie sent her a hesitant look. "Are you sure
about this? I mean, I could put the wedding off.
You know…until you finish grad school."

And the truth was that Lizzie would do that
if Jules asked her to make the sacrifice. She just
hated how insistent Lizzie was on her going to
grad school. Maybe now was the time to tell her
that she'd changed her mind. That she wasn't up
for any more school at this point in her life, and
that after doing an internship at the social services office, she knew that she wasn't cut out to
be a social worker. She just couldn't stuff her feelings in a box and do what was expected of her.

As it was, she'd spoken up one too many times
and was asked not to return. But she just couldn't
stand by and watch as government guidelines
overruled common sense. It was frustrating. In-
furiating. There had to be another way to help
deserving children in this world, and she hadn't

figured out how yet. But she would. One way or another.

"Lizzie, listen. About grad school, I was thinking—"

"That we haven't thrown you some sort of celebration." Lizzie smiled, and her eyes sparkled with happiness. "I'm sorry. I didn't mean to steal your thunder with the wedding and all."

"You didn't. Honest." The wedding was the best thing to happen as far as Jules was concerned. Her sister had more things to worry about than just her. "Getting married was something you and I never thought would happen for us. This is your chance to have a real family. You have to make the most of this—for both of us."

Lizzie hugged her tight, and Jules blinked repeatedly, trying to keep the tears from splashing onto her cheeks. She'd been kidding herself. Sure, gaining the freedom to make her own choices would be great, but the price of giving up this close relationship was almost more than she could bear.

Lizzie pulled back. "Does this mean that we're okay?"

Jules nodded while stuffing down the torrent of emotions churning inside her. She wouldn't ruin this for Lizzie. After all Lizzie had done for her, she deserved every bit of happiness she could find in this life.

"We're perfect. Now let's go see what the men are up to."

"Knowing those two, we might have to break up a sparring match."

Jules gaped. "They don't get along?"

"Oh, no. They get along. But when Stefano starts his big-brother routine, Dante takes matters into his own hands. They end up acting like two-year-olds." Lizzie smiled and shook her head. "If only Stefano would realize that Dante is all grown up now and not in need of his brotherly advice."

Jules wanted to say that it was like the pot calling the kettle black, but she refrained. She knew it all came from a special place in Lizzie's heart. And now wasn't the time to delve into that messy subject. It could wait until later.

CHAPTER SEVEN

THIS COULDN'T BE HAPPENING.

The next day, Stefano stood in the office of Ristorante Massimo while Dante took a business call. They'd just returned from getting measured for new tuxes while the women were out shopping. He figured with his one and only brother getting hitched, it was time to pull out all the stops. After all, it was his duty to look his best with Jules on his arm—for the ceremony, of course.

From the disgruntled tone of Dante's voice, the phone conversation wasn't going well. And the way his brother was frowning told him that his brother was losing the argument.

Dante slammed the phone down and turned to him. "Lizzie isn't going to like this. At all."

"She isn't going to like what?" Lizzie glided into the room and into Dante's arms as though they'd been together for years.

Stefano's gaze moved to Jules, who stood hesitantly in the doorway. He imagined what it'd be like for her to rush into his arms. He longed to pull her petite form to him. He inwardly groaned imagining her soft curves pressing against him.

Jules's eyes met his. Was that a questioning look? Was it possible she had caught on to his wayward thoughts?

Impossible. His guilty conscience was just getting to him. He had no business fantasizing about her—or anyone.

He turned to Dante and Lizzie, who'd drifted apart. The smiles had faded and a serious undercurrent ran through the room. He wished Dante would just spill the news instead of letting the tension mount. Then again, maybe Dante was waiting for some privacy to talk with Lizzie alone.

"Maybe we should go," Stefano said to Jules.

"Uh…" Her glance swung back and forth between Lizzie and Dante. "Okay. Call me."

"No, wait. This involves both of you. Might as well tell everyone at once. Close the door, Lizzie."

Without a word, she did as he asked, closing out the noise of the kitchen staff. Stefano straightened. This wasn't going to be good. Maybe this was the last straw for Dante. Perhaps the setbacks had made him realize that the DeFiore men weren't meant for marriage.

The bad part about all of this was that Stefano had grown to really like Lizzie. She had spunk and a fire in her that you just couldn't help but admire. And she was good for his brother. Just like Gianna had been good for him. She *had* been good for him, hadn't she? At some point, they had been good together…hadn't they?

The memories stuck a sword of guilt through his gut. Her death was on his hands. He may not have done it, but he was the cause of it. If only he had kept his mouth shut. If only they hadn't argued—

"Dante, you're worrying me." Lizzie stepped up to him. "What is it?"

"That was the studio on the phone."

"But didn't we just talk to them yesterday? I thought everything was settled."

"It was. And then the execs looked at the footage we filmed this past week for the upcoming series." Dante ran a hand over the back of his neck. "They don't like it. They say that it isn't fresh enough. They want to change the backdrop and the menus."

"What?" Lizzie stepped back. Her mouth fell open, and her eyes widened. "They can't do that."

"They can. And they have."

Well, this certainly wasn't the news Stefano was expecting. And he was surprised to feel a huge wave of relief. Though he believed his brother was headed for trouble, he didn't want to see him get hurt. It wasn't his place to say anything. Dante would have to make his own decisions—for better or worse—all by himself, just like Stefano had done with Gianna.

He relaxed and settled on the couch in the office. He didn't know why his brother had wanted him and Jules to stick around. She moved to the couch and sat down, too. Even at this respectable distance, she skewed his thinking. His only tangible thought was how her gentle floral scent reminded him of sunny days and grassy fields. And that was not good. He'd forfeited his right to enjoy a woman's presence the night Gianna had died.

"Do you have any idea why we're here?" Jules leaned closer to him.

"You're here because this impacts the wedding," Dante said before turning to Lizzie. "There's no way we can do what they want for the show and complete the wedding preparations in time."

Lizzie's hands settled on her hips. "But they said they wanted the wedding for the show."

"They said a lot of things, but we can't do everything. I'm sorry. We'll have to reschedule the wedding."

Stefano didn't want to say that this was an ominous sign—a warning—but he did think it was a chance for his brother to slow down and think through his choices. Still, the crushed look on Lizzie's face dug at him. They really didn't deserve so many problems, but it wasn't as if he could do anything to help.

"Are you saying you don't want to get married anymore?" Lizzie's voice wavered.

"Of course I do." Dante reached out and caressed her now pale cheek. "You know I love you. Maybe we can just make it something quick and simple."

Jules moved as if to stand up, and Stefano grabbed her arm, stopping her from interrupting. They really needed to figure this out for themselves. Certainly if there was such a serious problem between him and Jules, he'd want to figure it out for himself. Not that they'd ever be planning a wedding or anything.

When Jules's puzzled gaze turned to him, he shook his head. Her frosted lips pressed into a firm line, and her brows drew together. But she remained seated. Together they waited to see what their siblings would decide.

"But I have my dress picked out." Lizzie pulled away from Dante. "This isn't fair. This television show is messing everything up. We should quit."

"You're forgetting we signed a contract. And I don't think you really want to walk away from this. I see how you light up in front of the cameras. You're a natural."

Lizzie sighed, and her shoulders slumped. "But it's our wedding. What are we going to do?"

This time when Jules went to stand up, she gave Stefano the death stare when he reached out to her. Boy, that woman was as stubborn as she was beautiful. What exactly was she going to offer to this conversation? He had to admit that he was quite curious. Still, it wasn't for them to interfere.

Jules's mouth started to open, but he beat her to the punch. "Jules and I should be going. Let us know what you decide to do."

All eyes turned to him. There were also two sets of raised brows and one frown. Everyone's face held an unspoken accusation. What in the world had he said that was so bad?

"Don't mind him." Jules turned her back to him. "We're here to help you. I think the real question is, do you still want to go through with the ceremony as planned?"

Dante and Lizzie gazed into each other's eyes.

"Yes." They spoke in unison.

Somehow that answer did not come as a surprise to him. Love made people do foolish things and gave them the illusion that they could overcome anything. But there were some things in life that even love couldn't conquer.

"Then let me help." Jules pressed her hands to her slender hips.

Lizzie raised her brows. "What do you have in mind?"

"Do you trust me?" Jules looked directly at her sister.

"Of course."

"Good. Then let me take over your wedding for you. All you'll have to do is your final dress fitting and make sure you show up for the ceremony." Jules grinned at her sister, lightening the mood.

"But there's so much to do. We couldn't ask you to do it all yourself—"

"Why not? I am the maid of honor, you know. And this isn't my first time helping with a wedding. And you know how I enjoy organizing things."

Lizzie turned a questioning gaze to Dante. "What do you think?"

He shrugged. "Whatever makes you happy is fine by me."

Lizzie turned to Jules. "You'd really do this for us?"

"Consider it my wedding gift."

"And," Dante piped up, "I'm sure my brother can give you lots of help. He has great taste. Isn't that right, Stefano?"

All eyes turned to him. Stefano struggled not to choke on his own tongue. They wanted him to help with the wedding preparations? Were they serious? "I don't think that's a good idea."

That response only succeeded in gaining him

yet another round of frowns. He swallowed hard while keeping his chin high. He knew he was fighting a losing battle, but he just wasn't ready to concede to picking out flowers and whatever else went into a wedding.

Dante walked over and clapped him on the shoulder. "This experience will do you good. Maybe it'll give you some new ideas for your wine-tasting events."

Stefano resisted the urge to roll his eyes. His brother was really digging deep to come up with ideas of why he should waste his time planning some froufrou event. But he knew better than to vocalize his thoughts. He had no doubt that Jules and Lizzie would pounce on him like two lionesses going after fresh meat. Inwardly, he cringed at the thought.

"And what do you expect me to do about work at the vineyard while I'm out planning your nuptials?"

"I'm sure Papa won't mind taking over the vineyard in your absence."

"That's the second time you've said that. What do you know that I don't?"

"He's hinted that he's feeling a bit left out. Ever since Gianna's accident…well, um, you've been doing more and more of the work."

"And he told you this?" Then it all clicked into place. He recalled how Dante and their father had repaired their strained relationship. Their father must have confided his true feelings to Dante.

"All I'm saying is that you don't have to worry about the vineyard—it'll be handled. And I'm sure you don't want Jules to have to rely on public transportation when time is so vital."

Didn't his brother understand that it wasn't just the work? Planning a wedding would bring back unwanted memories. Thinking of Gianna still brought with it a truckload of guilt. If he hadn't married her and if he hadn't been expecting a life like the one his mother and father shared—a traditional lifestyle with the man working in the fields and the wife at home tending to the children—then maybe they wouldn't have started fighting. Maybe then she wouldn't have torn off in an angry huff that stormy night...

"I know Stefano won't let us down," Dante said confidently. "He's always there when the family needs him."

No, he wasn't. Otherwise he'd have been there for Gianna. But that was beside the point right now.

And so was how he felt about his brother tempting fate with this wedding. The only truly important thing now was that his brother was counting on him and he couldn't let him down. It'd been a long time since Dante had asked him for anything.

"Yeah, I'll help. As long as Papa is okay with the plan."

Dante smiled broadly. "Good. I'll call him as soon as we're done talking here."

Stefano couldn't believe he was going to help plan a wedding. Surely they didn't expect him to do more than drive Jules around. Even that would be a challenge. Though she was not his type, he couldn't deny her beauty. And those short skirts that she wore that showed off her toned legs were such a distraction. Jules's clothes were nothing like Gianna would have worn, no matter how modern his wife wanted to be. And what amazed him most was now that he'd gotten over the shock of Jules's trendy wardrobe, he was really starting to like the way she dressed.

But her makeup still made him pause. He wished she wouldn't apply it so heavily. He thought she was beautiful, but to be honest, it was hard to tell with all the makeup. And it taunted him, making him long to wipe it away and get to the real woman beneath it all.

The dresses were done. *Check.*

Well, not exactly. They were picked out, which in Jules's opinion was the hardest part of any wedding. Lizzie had her heart set on a stunning full-length oyster-colored gown. The fitted bodice was hand-beaded with crystal embellishments. The sweetheart neckline accentuated Lizzie's long neck, and the asymmetrical pleating that draped up over her waist was to die for. Jules thought it was absolutely perfect—befitting Cinderella herself.

For herself, they'd agreed on a knee-length strapless dress. The part she liked the best was the color: jazzberry jam. A black sash set off the whole dress and tied at the side. And they both agreed on a pair of black strappy sandals to go with it.

That was one thing she admired about her sister. Lizzie wasn't afraid of making decisions and going for it. She knew what she liked, and she didn't waver after her decision was made. Jules wished she was more like her. But maybe there was hope for her. Lately she'd noticed that she was more willing to make a decision without any input, and it felt good.

Armed with a wedding guide, a day planner and a credit card, Jules was ready to get to work. She glanced over at Stefano as he navigated his way through the congested streets of Rome.

"Is traffic always like this?" she asked.

"Like what?"

"So busy."

"Not always, but we've hit the morning commute. I told you we should have waited a bit before coming to the city."

She shifted uncomfortably in the leather seat. "I thought you were just putting me off because you didn't want to come with me."

"Why would you think that? I agreed to help, didn't I?"

She glanced down at her black-and-white plaid miniskirt. It was the tamest thing she owned. For the first time she felt out of place. The truth was she used her clothes as a defense mechanism. If people were busy talking about the length of her hemline, they weren't noticing how the heavy makeup camouflaged her facial scars.

But right now she wondered what it would be like to let down her guard and dress like everyone else—like Lizzie. It would definitely be different. Maybe it'd make Stefano less hesitant to escort her around Rome. It was a thought. One she'd take into consideration. She just wasn't so sure that she was ready to let down her tightly held defenses just yet.

"I…I just know that your brother gave you a healthy shove into agreeing to this."

"Here's a lesson in DeFiore men. When we don't want to do something, we don't do it. And nothing and no one will change our minds."

She took in his serious expression. Maybe she was reading too much into his reluctance to leave the vineyard that morning. Perhaps she should have believed him when he'd said he didn't want to get stuck with the morning commuters.

But she still found herself thinking of visiting a boutique or two while they were shopping. She couldn't afford off-the-rack fashions. Unlike her sister, who shopped at secondhand stores, Jules found most of her stuff at the back of stores on the clearance racks. When your tastes were a bit eclectic, it made discount shopping a lot easier. But that would have to wait. She had other, more important, business to deal with first.

"I was just going over the wedding checklist, and we might just pull this off."

"Might?" He chanced a quick glance her way.

"Well, yes. It's going to be a lot of work, but we already have the venue and the dresses, and Lizzie found a place online that will print her invitations and mail them for her. Those will go out this week. Let's see. What else is there?" Her gaze skimmed down over the master list. "Lizzie mentioned something about you being able to supply tables and chairs."

Stefano nodded. "We have plenty we keep on hand for large events at the winery."

"Great." One more thing checked off her long list. "Are we almost at the next florist?"

"Yes, it's right ahead." Stefano braked for a traffic light. "I still don't know what you didn't like about the last florist."

She turned a narrowed gaze his way. "They were trying to pawn their overstock on us. They wanted to make an easy sale, and I don't want that. Lizzie and Dante deserve more than that. Lizzie and I don't exactly come from a traditional background. And now that she's found her Prince Charming, she—they—deserve to have a perfect day. And if that takes you and I driving all around this city to find the right florist, then that's what we'll do."

"I didn't know you were that invested in this wedding."

"There's a lot about me that you don't know."

"I'm listening if you want to tell me."

For a moment, she was tempted to let down her guard and open up to him about the loss of her mother and the string of foster homes. But what would that accomplish? Nothing. She had to stay focused. "This isn't about me. It's about Lizzie and Dante."

The traffic surged forward, and Stefano followed. "It doesn't look like there's any parking. I'll drop you off. You have my cell number, right?"

"Yes, but aren't you coming in?"

"The last time you were in and out so fast that I'd just walked up in time to hold the door as you stormed out—"

"I wasn't that bad. Was I?"

A smile tugged at his lips. "Let's just say that everyone knew you weren't a satisfied customer."

"But what if these people don't speak English? You have to come with me. After all, you told your brother that you would help with everything. You don't want to go back on your word, do you?" Jules reached down and grabbed her oversize purse, which contained pictures of the dresses and color swatches. Without waiting for his response, she added, "I'll see you inside."

CHAPTER EIGHT

WHAT IN THE world had his brother gotten him into?

Stefano's feet felt weighted down as he made his way to the florist. The last thing he needed to be doing was escorting Jules around. She made him think things and feel things he shouldn't. And when she looked at him with those big green eyes, his common sense took a hike. His raging hormones took charge and left him longing to steal a kiss. A long, passionate one.

He was in so much trouble.

He half hoped Jules would already be waiting for him on the sidewalk. They could head back to the villa, and he could lose himself in his work. It'd keep his mind from straying back to Jules's sultry lips or tempting butterfly. He inwardly groaned.

And no matter what Dante said about his father wanting to get more involved with the business side of things, Stefano had made a lot of changes since his father had last run DeFiore Winery. Stefano was certain he'd have questions.

When Stefano neared the front of the shop, he peered in the big showroom window. Colorful blooms in various arrangements stared back at him, and he saw no sign of Jules making a hasty exit. Could it be that this place lived up to her high standards?

He sighed in relief. Once they placed a quick order, they'd be back on the road. Maybe this day wasn't going to be a complete waste of time after all.

A little bell above the door chimed as he entered the shop. He was surprised to find so many people inside. There were men with bouquets of long-stemmed red roses. Others had arrangements of pink carnations. And yet another man had a bouquet of lilies, some sort of bright green pom-poms, brilliant pink roses and tiny deep purple flowers. And then there were a cluster of young women pointing at the cooler cases that held a wide array of flowers in black buckets. He couldn't help but wonder if this place was always this busy. Perhaps he'd gone into the wrong business.

He found Jules at the back of the shop, studying a cooler case of flowers he didn't recognize. "Did you find what you need?"

"I think so."

"Good." This had gone even easier than he'd imagined. "Ready to go?"

"Go? Are you kidding?" When she looked at him with those big green eyes, he could feel himself melting. "I haven't even talked with a salesperson yet."

"You haven't? What have you been doing?" It wasn't until the words were out of his mouth that he realized how they sounded.

She frowned. "You might get things done by pushing to the front of the line, but there are those of us who believe in waiting our turn."

His head lowered. She was right. "I just didn't realize there'd be such a demand for flowers." Well, he wasn't going to do any good just standing there taking up space. "It looks like it's going to be a while. I've got some things to do. I'll be back—"

"You're leaving me?"

The way she said it made him feel as though he was shirking his duties as best man. "I was just trying to make good use of the time. I don't know a dandelion from a carnation."

"You can help me pick out some flowers. Lizzie told me the main flower she wants in her bouquet is a dahlia. If possible it should have a yellow center with deep pink tips. She said they have a sentimental meaning for her and Dante." Jules shrugged her slender shoulders. "I see that they have some here, so it shouldn't be too much of a problem to get them to order more. I hope."

"Great. It sounds like you have the flowers all figured out." He turned toward the door, feeling extremely uncomfortable as a grandmotherly woman gave him a smile and a nod as though she thought that Jules and he were…were a couple. "I'll just wait outside."

Jules reached out and caught his arm. "Not so fast. I still need some other flowers to complement the bouquet. I thought about baby's breath, but everyone uses that. Lizzie needs something different. Something that will make the colors in the bouquet pop. You know this whole thing will be on television. Well, not the whole thing, but highlights of the wedding. And it just has to be perfect."

Stefano stifled a groan as Jules pulled him around to look at the variety of flowers. Though she mainly wore black and white, she appeared to have a fondness for other colors, too. *Interesting*.

"I'm sorry it took me a bit to get to you two." The saleswoman was an older lady who spoke perfect English with an Italian accent. "With summer here, romance is in the air."

"It certainly is." Jules smiled broadly. "We're here to order flowers for a wedding."

Stefano was caught off guard by the ease of her smile and the twinkle in her eyes. Was it possible that Jules was a closet romantic? She certainly seemed to know enough about this stuff.

The woman's face lit up. "What do you have in mind?"

Jules turned to him and asked if he'd hold her purse. He quickly scanned the area. Relieved to find no male witnesses, he reached out for the very large black leather purse. He was shocked by its weight. What did she carry in there? Barbells?

He watched as Jules opened her wedding planner and flipped to a page with colorful pictures, but before he could focus in on the images, she lifted the notebook out of his view. Whether it was intentional or not, he didn't know and he wasn't about to ask. He didn't need her thinking that he was interested in any of it. He was doing his duty as best man. Nothing more.

The saleswoman produced various stems of tiny flowers from white to pink to deep purple. In the beginning, Jules would turn to consult him. He generally shrugged and said they were nice. After he kept repeating the same response, she gave up asking for his input, which was fine with him.

"Don't worry, honey." The woman patted Jules's arm. "If it were up to most men, they'd pick some wildflowers from the side of the road as a wedding bouquet. That's why you have me."

"Thank you so much. I really appreciate all of

your help. And I know it's short notice, but the wedding is next month. Will we be able to get the flowers in time for the ceremony?"

"Let me check." The woman pulled out a day planner and Jules read off the date. "*Non c'è problema*. You two are such a cute couple." The woman beamed at them.

Without warning, Jules leaned over, wrapped her hands around his arm and leaned her head against his shoulder. His body stiffened. What was she doing? He would have asked, but his heart in his throat kept him from breathing, much less speaking.

"You really think so?" Jules lifted her chin and smiled broadly up at him.

"Oh, definitely. Just wait until you have children. They'll be real darlings."

"Hmm…I hadn't thought about it."

Jules gave him a quick once-over as though inspecting his physical attributes to see if he would make good father material—a father to their children. When her gaze met his, her lips lifted into a smile that lit up her eyes. His jaw tightened. She was having fun at his expense. But what bothered him the most was he could easily envision a little girl with Jules's big green eyes—his daughter. He stopped his thoughts from meandering down that dangerous path.

What in the world was going on? He and Jules

were barely even friends, much less planning a life together. That was not going to happen.

Jules pulled away. Although he should have felt relieved, he found himself missing her touch. It killed him to admit even to himself, but he'd enjoyed the softness of her hands pressing against his bare arm. The warmth of her gaze was powerful stuff. A man could get swept away and forget all about logic. He'd have to be careful around this one. He wasn't going to fall in love again. No way. The price was too high.

The saleswoman continued to beam at them. "Don't you two worry about flowers for your big day. As soon as I looked at you I knew there was a love connection. You'll make a wonderful bride and groom."

Stefano cleared his throat, at last feeling as though he'd regained his ability to speak—he must clear up this misunderstanding. He couldn't continue to play along with Jules's game any longer.

"We aren't together." His voice came out gruff.

Both women turned to him with startled looks. It had to be from the tone of his voice because there was no way that Jules was surprised by his admission. It wasn't as if she even liked him.

Did she?

"This isn't for our wedding." Stefano had to correct the woman since Jules didn't seem the least bit interested in doing it. He couldn't let the woman go on about them being such a great couple.

Jules's perfectly plucked brows drew together into a formidable line and her lush red lips pressed together as though she were holding back a heated reprimand. Let her fume. He'd merely corrected a glaring error. End of story.

The saleswoman's puzzled gaze moved from him to Jules. "I don't understand." The woman's face took on a very serious expression. "These flowers you've picked out, if they aren't for you two, who are they for?"

Jules sent him a this-is-your-fault look. But he didn't feel the least bit guilty. Why should he?

She shifted her weight in those sky-high black-heeled boots that made her look as if she'd just stepped out of some rock-and-roll video. Not that he'd watched many. But he had seen a few in his time, and, well, she was definitely gorgeous enough to star in them if only she'd lighten up on the makeup so people could really see her. But right now there was no mistaking that she was upset. Not even that thick makeup could hide her frown lines.

Jules clasped her hands together. "The thing is we're picking out flowers for another couple."

"You're what?" The saleswoman looked taken aback. "Where's the bride?"

"Working. She had an emergency come up and asked if we'd step in and help with the plans."

"Will she be in later to approve the order?"

"I'm afraid not." Jules clenched her hands together.

"I don't think we can take your order—"

"But you must." Jules's voice cracked with emotion. "We're running out of options. I promise everything will be to the bride's liking."

The saleswoman shook her head. "We can't do it."

"What's the big deal?" Stefano came to Jules's defense. "They're flowers, for goodness' sake. They all pretty much look the same except for the colors. And Jules showed you the color of the dresses. Now we'd like to buy some flowers."

"You might want to, but that doesn't mean it's going to happen. Listen, I just got burned on a really big order where the bride was too busy with her dress or some such thing to come in and approve what her mother picked out for the wedding. I'm still sorting out that mess." She shook her head. "I'm not doing that again. Either the bride comes in or you'll have to go elsewhere to buy your flowers."

The woman couldn't be serious. He glanced at Jules, who looked upset. "Listen here, you can't do that—"

"What he meant to say is we understand.

Thank you so much for your time." She pulled on his arm to leave.

He refused to be turned away. "I want to talk to the owner."

The saleswoman pressed her hands to her generous hips. "You're speaking to her. And it's time you left."

"Thanks again." Jules tugged harder and finally he gave in, letting her lead him from the flower shop. He didn't know why she was retreating. The woman was there to sell flowers and they were there to buy them, not cater to the woman's wishes. This was ridiculous.

Once outside and down the sidewalk a ways, Jules spun around and got in his face with her finger pointing at him. Her face was filled with color. Her eyes narrowed on him. This wasn't going to be pretty. Not at all.

"Do you know what you just did in there?" Her heated tone left no doubt about her agitation.

"Yes, I corrected the woman. You let her think that we were a couple. I couldn't let her think that."

"Why? Is it so awful to think that you and I might be involved?"

He rubbed the back of his neck, trying to avoid the curious looks as people passed by. "Can we talk about this later? People are starting to stare."

"Let them. You owe me some answers."

"Fine. I don't like to lie. And letting that woman believe we're something we're not was a lie."

Jules's gaze narrowed even more. "And you are the pillar of honesty?"

He lowered his head as memories of his not so distant past started to pound him. No, he wasn't the pillar of anything. In fact, he was the exact opposite. If he'd been more of a proponent of the truth while he was married, he might still be married—well, he wouldn't go that far. But Gianna would still be alive.

He'd give anything to erase that awful night. Anything at all.

"Lying only leads to regrets." He looked at Jules. She didn't seem as hostile now. In fact, the way she was gazing at him it was as if she was trying to read him. "What does any of this matter, anyway? They were just flowers. I'm sure there are lots of other shops that would be more than willing to take our business."

"Not if you keep shooting your mouth off like that. These people like to know that they are dealing with the person in charge—"

"And that's you—"

"Not in this case. This is a wedding. The bride is always in charge. It's her wedding. Her big day. The whole thing revolves around her. And these people have been down the aisle enough times to know how it works."

"So if that's the case, why's Lizzie dumping it all in your lap instead of delaying the wedding?"

"Because she trusts me. We're the only family each other has. We know each other better than anyone in the world, and she knows that I will plan the perfect wedding for her."

"I hope you're right. About knowing her so well."

Jules's lips lifted in a small smile. "You don't have to worry." She lifted her phone and waved it in his face. "I've been texting and sending photos on top of talking to her every day. She's on top of things. I'm just acting as her mouthpiece."

That bit of news sent a wave of relief through him. But they still had to find flowers, someplace without such a picky saleswoman.

"Well, Ms. Mouthpiece, any ideas where we should go next?"

"I don't know. Let me see." She started typing on her smartphone.

When she turned to start walking, he called out, "You're going the wrong way."

She glanced up, confusion reflected in her beautiful eyes. "Oh."

Quietly they retraced their steps. Her focus was on her phone. And his attention was on keeping her from walking into other pedestrians. When they reached the car, she had another florist for them to try. But it was nearing lunchtime, and he really needed a break before they set out again.

He turned to Jules. "How about lunch?"

"Already?" When she glanced at the time on her phone, her lips formed an O. "I didn't realize it was so late. Would you mind if we had lunch at Ristorante Massimo? I have a couple of things to go over with Lizzie."

"Sounds like a plan. Why don't you call ahead? Dante can have something waiting for us so it won't take so long. Those two stops this morning took forever. I hope we don't have to wait that long in the next shop." He didn't know if he had the patience for this wedding shopping. It was like watching a grape ripen—painfully slow.

"I hope so, too, or the shopping is going to take us more than a week. And with time being of the essence, we have to move quickly. We still have the cake to pick out."

"Why didn't we do that first?"

Jules grinned at him. "Because the cake tasting is the best part of this whole adventure. It's like a reward."

He smiled and shook his head. "I don't know how someone as slender as you can gorge on cake."

"You just watch, and I'll show you." Her eyes twinkled with mischief.

Jules was a breath of fresh air. She was nothing

like the women that lived in the nearby village, who enjoyed a more sedate way of life. And yet she wasn't like some of the posh urban women who attended the wine-tasting events and were always in such a hurry. Jules had an air about her, but it was all her own.

The more time he spent with her, the more he was beginning to like her—really like her. And that just couldn't happen.

CHAPTER NINE

A DELICIOUS LUNCH could change one's perspective.

If Jules had known food could put a smile on Stefano's face, she'd have suggested it ages ago. He'd actually started a conversation, but it was directed at Dante, not her. And it was about one of his favorite subject—grapes. Still it had been nice watching him let down his guard and relax.

But as soon as they climbed back in the car, the walls around him went back up, blocking her out. She didn't understand what she'd done to get him to hold her at arm's length. Surely he still wasn't upset about the salesclerk thinking they were a couple.

Jules glanced down at her black skirt, black stockings and black boots. Okay, so maybe her color choice was a bit somber, but her styles weren't.

She gave herself a mental jerk. What was she doing? Reevaluating her clothes because of a guy that barely tolerated her? She was fine just the way she was. And black was her favorite color.

She needed to focus on the wedding, not pleasing Stefano. With that thought, she realized it might be best to tell him exactly what she had in mind as they visited this florist.

She leaned over and said, "Just follow my lead. Can you do that?"

He maneuvered the car into a parking spot. "Depends. Are you going to lie?"

"Stefano, do you want this wedding to be nice for your brother?"

"Yes, but he isn't going to care about flowers."

"He might not, but his bride will. If she's not happy, do you really think that he'll be happy?"

There was a strained pause. "I suppose not."

She didn't say a word as he alighted from the car. While she gathered her purse and wedding planner, Stefano rounded the front of the car. She reached for the door handle, but Stefano beat her to it and swung it open. He was a gentleman, something she wasn't accustomed to. But she could get used to this. After all, if they were about to create a little bit of make-believe, she might as well enjoy some of the benefits.

Inside there was one man working the shop, and he was already busy with someone at the register placing an order. That would give her time to scope out his supply and find out if he was a viable candidate.

"Oh, look—they have dahlias." She rushed over to take a closer look. "And there are some in the right color." She couldn't resist smiling and gently clapped her hands. "So far, so good."

Stefano pretended to be interested, but she could tell by his reserved reaction that he was less than impressed. She wasn't going to let his mood ruin this for her. She intended to enjoy this wedding as much as possible. It was quite possibly the last thing that Lizzie would ever ask her to do...especially after Lizzie learned that she wasn't going to grad school.

"Are you finding what you're looking for?" The salesman approached them.

This was where she had to play her cards just right. There was no way she was going through all the pain and effort to select the flowers only to have the man turn them away. They didn't have the time to waste.

She slipped her hand in Stefano's. When he tried to pull away, she tightened her grip. Silently she willed him to play along with her. She would do her best not to outright lie. The impression the salesman made would be his own responsibility.

After all, she certainly wasn't expecting anything to come of this. Sure, she'd dated in the past, but she'd always insisted on keeping things casual—except one time. It had been a blind date set up by her lab partner. His name was J.T. It had been a case of infatuation from the get-go. As they'd started to see each other on a regular basis, she'd thought they were building the solid foundation for a committed relationship. She had been certain of it.

With J.T's graduation just weeks away, he'd asked her to dinner. He'd said that he had something he wanted to say to her. She recalled how excited she'd been. While Lizzie had done her utmost to talk sense into her, all Jules could think about was a diamond ring. At last, someone in her life who would love her and never leave.

In the end, the dinner had been a thank-you for tutoring him in a philosophy class. He had told her that he couldn't have passed the course without her help. And, as she'd tried her best to suck up her disappointment, he'd capped off the evening with an announcement that he was moving across the country to California. He was leaving, and she wasn't invited to go with him.

It wasn't until after a couple of tissue boxes—the jumbo size—that she had realized it had worked out for the best. It reaffirmed her belief that love didn't exist. It was a fleeting notion. Something that she never planned to explore ever again. But now, after witnessing Lizzie and

Dante's relationship, she thought maybe her assessment hadn't been quite so accurate.

Jules presented her best smile to the salesman. "We'd like to order some flowers for a wedding."

"Excellent." The man glanced around as though searching for something. "Let me just grab something to write on." He rushed back to the counter and returned with a clipboard and a pen. "When is the wedding?"

"The middle of next month."

The smile faded from the man's face. "Oh, that soon."

"Is that a problem?"

"Why don't you tell me what you have in mind, and we'll go from there."

Not wanting to press her luck, she released Stefano's hand. She chanced a quick glance at him to find a frown pulling at his lips. Disappointment wiped away her own smile. Not exactly the look a bride would want from her intended bridegroom, but it wasn't as if they were even involved. So then why did his scowl dig at her?

After reviewing each flower on Lizzie's list, the man assured her he'd be able to order them all. The bridal bouquet would be quite extravagant. And the changes the florist suggested, although small, were just enough to set off the flowers.

With the deposit made, Jules and Stefano turned to the door. She slipped her hand back in his. She didn't have to, she knew that, but she wanted to feel his strong fingers entwined with hers. It had been a long time since she'd dated. Maybe she was lonelier than she'd thought. Or maybe all of this focus on the wedding was making her realize how alone she'd be without her sister.

"Don't worry," the salesman called out. "You two will have a marvelous wedding."

She turned and waved goodbye. His words drove home her loneliness. Maybe always being the bridesmaid wasn't all she'd convinced herself it would be.

Jules sucked in an unsteady breath. She'd promised herself on the flight over that she wouldn't fall apart. She would be happy for her foster sister. No matter what.

"Are you okay?" Stefano stopped on the sidewalk to look at her.

"Umm…yes, I'm fine." When she realized that her hand was still in his, she tried to pull away, but this time he was the one to tighten his grip.

She gave up the struggle and took comfort in the innocent touch. Instead of dwelling on her loneliness, she turned her thoughts back to Apricot. She desperately wanted to take the kitten home with her. She'd soon be known as the spinster cat lady, she mused. She wondered what Stefano would say if he knew about the direction of her pathetic thoughts.

As for the kitten, she wasn't so sure it was a good idea to transport it such a long distance. And if she didn't know better, she'd swear that Apricot was working her way into Stefano's heart. Perhaps finding Apricot a home wouldn't be as hard as she'd originally thought.

She still had a handful of weeks until the wedding to make up her mind about the cat. One way or another Apricot would have a loving home.

More than a week had passed since the whirlwind, otherwise known as Jules, had blown Stefano's routine life off course. Nothing was the same with her around. She'd befriended his father. Nonno thought the sun rose around her. And Maria had taken her under her wing, showing her some of her favorite recipes. It was as though Jules fit right in.

But she didn't belong at the vineyard. And she never would. Nothing good would come of him imagining any other scenario.

So if that was the case, why had he immediately noticed Jules's absence from the breakfast table? He forced himself to stay there and eat. After all, she wasn't his responsibility. It was enough that he had to babysit her on their numerous ventures to Rome, but the line had to be drawn somewhere. He couldn't risk getting involved.

Once he'd finished his *caffè*, he quietly emptied his barely picked-over breakfast into the trash. He had no appetite even though Maria was a fine cook. At last he escaped to the silence of the outdoors, but it was no easy task. His father was in quite a chatty mood. In fact, he hadn't seen his father this animated in a long time. Maybe Dante had been right. Maybe Stefano had unintentionally cut his father out of more of the business than he'd intended. At least one of them was happy.

Once outside, Stefano hesitated. His thoughts turned back to Jules. Maybe he should check on her. After all, something could be wrong. He assured himself that it was his duty to be a good host. With his mind made up, he made his way around to the front of the house, preferring to avoid the prying eyes in the kitchen.

In no time at all, he was standing outside Jules's room. He rapped his knuckles on the door. "Jules, are you there?"

"Come in."

He didn't know what to expect when he opened the door, but it wasn't the sight that greeted him. There was Jules sitting on the floor, surrounded by an array of various shades of purple-and-white tissue paper. And the kitten was scurrying around, chasing bits of paper. What a mess.

In the middle of it all, Jules smiled up at him. "Hi. Did you need something?"

"I didn't see you at breakfast. I thought maybe you weren't feeling well."

"No, I'm fine. I'm just busy." She held up a tissue-paper flower for his inspection. "What do you think?"

"Um…" He wasn't so sure what to say. "It's nice."

Her smile broadened. "Thanks. I'm a bit of an expert at these by now. But I've never had to make them by myself before. Usually the bridal party gets together for some fun and we make the flowers. By the end of the night, there's hundreds of them. But since Lizzie wants a small wedding, I guess it's up to me to make them."

"But I don't understand. Isn't that what we went to the florist for?" He'd never figure out women, no matter how long he lived.

"This is different. These are for decorations."

"If we need to buy more flowers, just say so." By the looks of this room, she'd been here for-ever making flowers.

"Thanks. But it's not necessary. I want both types of flowers."

This wedding business was way more involved than he'd imagined. Jules was going to wear her-self to a frazzle. There had to be a better way to go about it. And that's where he could help her out.

"You can't do everything yourself."

With a paper punch in one hand and tissue paper in the other, she paused and glanced up at him. "Why, Stefano, is that your way of offering to make flowers with me?"

"Definitely not." When her smile dimmed, he hurried to correct himself. "I mean, I can hire someone to do this stuff. I can hire as many people as it takes. Just tell me what you need."

Jules unfolded her legs and stood. "I don't want strangers doing Lizzie's wedding."

He was obviously missing something, but he had no clue what it might be. Back when he was married to Gianna when he didn't understand her logic, he'd just shrug and walk away. Maybe if he'd asked more questions and tried to understand her better, their life wouldn't have careened out of control.

"Why in the world not?"

"It doesn't matter."

Okay, he probably could have worded that better. He cleared his throat to try again. "Talk to me. Obviously there's something I'm missing and I'd like to understand."

Surprise reflected in her green gaze. "I...I don't have money to buy them a proper wedding gift. I know it's silly, but I want to create a cozy wedding with a personal touch. Lizzie doesn't know I'm doing all of this. And don't you tell her."

He felt like such an unfeeling lowlife now. The money aspect had never even crossed his mind. And he had to admit Jules's gift would surpass even the most expensive offering because it came from the heart.

"Your gift will be their favorite." And he meant it. "What can I do to help, aside from making flowers? I don't think mine would be suitable for anything but the garbage."

Jules's stance eased, and she asked if she could use his computer to order some favors. She listed off things he never would have thought of, including wedding bubbles and sparklers. It would definitely be a wedding to remember.

"You're welcome to use my computer anytime. Now, how about taking a break to eat?"

She settled back on the floor, right in the middle of the mess. "I'll get to it later. I'm excited to see how many of these I can get done today. And Apricot is being a big help."

Stefano looked dubiously at the kitten running around and batting at the scraps of colorful tissue paper. Well, as long as Jules was happy, he was fine with it.

"I've got some work at the barn that I need to do. If you need me, I'll be there."

She gathered a stack of tissue paper and pushed

a round punch through the sheets. "We're good. Huh, Apricot?"

The kitten gave her a quick glance and then returned to playing.

Stefano felt guilty as he walked away. But seriously, having him make tissue-paper flowers would have been an utter disaster. Maybe he could help with her internet shopping. That was something he could do.

With a plan in mind, his steps toward the barn grew quicker. She didn't want help from strangers, but that didn't include him. They'd moved past being strangers a while back. Where they were headed he wasn't quite sure.

He walked into the office just in time to find his father shutting down the computer. "Calling it a day already?"

Papa jerked his salt-and-pepper head up. "Sorry. I didn't hear you come in. Umm…yes. I thought I'd take a break."

"You feeling all right?"

"Of course." Frown lines creased Papa's tanned face. "Am I that much of a workaholic that you think because I am out of the office something must be wrong?"

Since when did his father become so defensive?

Stefano shrugged, trying to take a neutral stance. "Is there anything around here that needs my immediate attention?"

His father rubbed his jaw. Instead of the gray stubble that normally dotted it, it was clean shaven. "Not that I can think of. I've calculated the number of new barrels we'll need for the fall harvest, and I've ordered the supplies. They should be here in a few weeks."

"What about the email? Is it backed up? It always seems they come in faster than I can respond to them."

"No, I just finished responding to the last email. Things are pretty quiet right now. I was thinking that perhaps we should consider increasing the number of wine-tasting events we host. It'd be good for the business, and I think it'd be well received."

Stefano nodded. "You know we have one coming up before the wedding."

"I do. I just think that we can do more."

It'd been one of those things that he'd been meaning to get to, but there was always something else that needed his attention first. But it seemed his father was on top of everything. Good for him. Right now, Stefano was actually kind of enjoying this downtime.

"You headed out to the fields?" Stefano asked, feeling obligated to accompany him. "I can give you a hand."

Papa's bushy brows rose. "Um…no, that isn't

necessary. I'm going to have some *caffè* first. Why don't you take the day off?"

That was the problem; he didn't want to slow down because then his thoughts would take over and that would do nothing but get him in trouble. He'd start remembering his past mistakes. Or worse yet, he'd start thinking about Jules in all the wrong ways. The last thing he needed to do was to start caring about her.

His father clapped him on the shoulder. "It's a beautiful day. Don't spend all of it in here."

After his father walked away, Stefano sat down at the desk. Out of the corner of his eye, he spied the coffeemaker. It was still on, and the pot was full. *What in the world?* Why was his father heading to the house for *caffè* when there was plenty here?

Stefano shook his head and gave up trying to figure out his father. He turned on the computer and found the email was in fact under control. The office was in decent shape. And there was absolutely no business requiring his attention. *Good.* Now he had time to help Jules with the wedding. His fingers flew over the keypad.

A little later, he headed back to the house, excited to tell Jules what he'd ordered. His steps grew faster the more he thought of her sitting on the floor in those short shorts with her bare legs showing and that contagious smile on her face.

He didn't know what it was about her that drew him in. She was unlike any other woman he'd ever known.

Maybe his problem was he spent too much time alone at this vineyard. But that was his punishment for what had happened to Gianna. He didn't let himself go out and have a good time. He didn't let himself think about the future because she didn't have one.

However, now, for the first time since his wife's tragic death, he wanted to live again. He wanted to feel alive. And that's how Jules made him feel—heart-poundingly, soul-stirringly alive.

It was a strange sensation after living so long in self-imposed exile. He'd cut himself off from most of the outside world. He'd unknowingly followed in his father's footsteps, even though he'd sworn that he would be different. Yet another thing he'd failed at, but he wouldn't fail Jules. He'd do his best to help her make this wedding special.

As he drew close to the house, he saw someone exit the kitchen door. It was Maria, and she was laughing. In the past eleven or so years that she'd been tending to the house, he didn't recall ever hearing her laugh like that—unrestricted and joyous. What could have put her in such a good mood—

His father.

Papa's deep chuckle drifted through the air. Stefano came to a halt. What in the world was going on?

Stefano watched in amazement as the two, not noticing him, started off toward the vines as though they were going for a stroll—together. If he hadn't seen it with his own eyes, he never would have believed his father was interested in Maria. How long had this been going on? And how had he missed it until now?

Did this explain the recent change in his father? The easiness Papa had taken on? The not working until all hours of the night? The added pep in his step?

Stefano raked his fingers through his hair as he tried to come to terms with the fact his father was back among the living. There was a mixed ball of emotions churning in his gut. He truly wanted to be happy for his father, but it nagged at him that he and his brother had suffered through their childhoods with an emotionally detached father. If only his father had made this change long ago, he could have saved everyone so much misery.

When his father and Maria were far enough off, Stefano made the rest of his way to the house. It seemed as though everyone was getting on with their lives—except him. But how did he do that? How did he forget what he'd done?

He didn't have any answers, just more questions. The one thing he could do was get into the spirit of his brother's wedding. Maybe Dante was right to roll the dice and see what life handed him.

The thought of Jules making all those silly paper flowers alone tugged at his conscious. He was the best man. And since there was no other bridal party, it fell to him to help her. Whether he was any good at it or not, he could try his best.

Spending some time with Jules was not silly—not at all. Besides, it would keep his mind off the fact that his father was changing—right before his very eyes. Suddenly Stefano felt as though he was standing still in life and soon he'd be left behind.

CHAPTER TEN

JULES RAN THE brush through her damp hair, pulling the dark strands back in a single ponytail. The cool shower felt rejuvenating. She'd just sat down on the bedroom floor to make some more flowers when there was a knock at the door.

Her chest tightened. She wasn't expecting anyone to come looking for her. She thought everyone was out and about doing their own thing.

She scrambled to her feet. The door was locked, so it wasn't like anyone would just come walking in on her.

"Jules, are you in there?" Stefano's deep tones vibrated through the door.

"Did you need something?"

"I have news. You know, it's easier to talk when there isn't a piece of wood standing between us."

Jules pressed her hands to her cheeks. She hadn't had a chance to do her makeup yet. She couldn't have him seeing her like this—with her scars exposed. Her heart beat rapidly. She didn't think she could stand to have him turn away in repulsion.

She stepped closer to the door. "Could we talk at lunch?"

There was a slight pause. "Is everything okay?"

What could be so important? She didn't have a clue. She had to admit that she was quite curious to know what was so urgent.

"Jules?" The doorknob jiggled. "Jules, what's going on? Why is your door locked?"

She sighed. He wasn't going to just give up and go away. She'd already witnessed his stubborn streak at the florist. This time he might just break down the door to see for himself that she was okay.

This might be just what she needed to end the silly crush she had on him. Once he saw the scars on her face, he'd turn tail and run.

"Jules, come on. You're starting to worry me."

She sucked in a steadying breath, leveled her shoulders and released the lock on the door. With a twist of the knob, she pulled it open. Stefano stood there, all six-plus feet of him, with his forehead wrinkled with worry lines. He stepped into the room, and she backed up so he could enter the whole way.

"See, nothing to worry about." She felt a little off center that he was actually worried about her. Aside from Lizzie, no one worried about her.

His gaze slid over her fuzzy black robe with purple polka dots. She suddenly wished it was a little longer. As it was, it barely reached midthigh, and the only thing beneath it was a lacy black bra and matching undies. Though she was modestly covered, she still felt fully exposed. She lowered her head, staring at her purple toenails.

"You aren't dressed yet?"

She shrugged. "I've been busy."

"I noticed. That's what I wanted to talk to you about—"

"If this is about hiring help, I told you to forget it."

"Actually, what I wanted to say is I know in the beginning I wasn't a fan of helping with this wedding, but I want to help now. I want to do whatever it is that you need. Just give me a task, and I'll get it done. Or at least I'll try my best."

Jules crossed her arms. "Do you mind if I ask what brought about this change of heart?"

He paused and stared at her. Was it her scars? Did he at last see her defects? That crescent moon scar that wrapped around the side of her left eye and the long scar that trailed down her jaw. They were so ugly.

She couldn't stand him staring any longer. She felt as though she were under a spotlight. Pretending to be intent on picking up some of her flower-making supplies from the floor, she kept her back to him.

"I'm sorry. I didn't mean to stare."

"I should have put on my makeup, but I didn't get to it yet."

"Don't." When she turned a questioning look his way, he added, "Don't put the makeup on."

She straightened and turned to him. "You've got to be kidding."

"No, I think you look beautiful without all of that stuff."

He couldn't be serious. There was no way someone could find her scarred face beautiful. She shook her head. "Don't lie."

"I'm not." He stepped closer to her. When she wouldn't meet his gaze, his thumb moved beneath her chin and raised her face until she was looking directly at him. "You are beautiful."

"But…but what about my scars?"

"The one by your eye is hardly noticeable. It's your green eyes that draw my attention. The gold flecks in them catch the light just right. And your pert nose is just perfect. And then there's your lips—they are quite fascinating. They look as though they are just ripe for kissing."

The breath hitched in her throat. He was seducing her with his words. No one had ever done that before, and all she wanted him to do now was put some action behind his compliments.

Then in the next breath his hand pulled away from her chin, and he stepped back. "If that's the only reason you wear all of that makeup, then don't. You are much more beautiful without it. Trust me. I wouldn't lie to you."

Maybe he wouldn't. He'd just lead her on and then leave her wanting a kiss that wasn't coming. How in the world was she ever going to concentrate on anything but him?

"I'll consider it." She'd been wearing makeup since she was a teen, hiding her scars.

"Are you still making flowers?" He glanced around at the array of papers on the floor.

"The shower gave me renewed energy, and I thought I might make some more before lunch."

"I see your helper faded away."

"Apricot wore herself out chasing the paper and then sliding across the floor. When she got bored of that I rolled a piece into a ball. She batted it everywhere until at last it went under the bed. Instead of going after it, she clawed her way up the bedspread and laid down."

There in the middle of her bed, in a pink fuzzy blanket Jules had bundled up into a circle with a divot in the middle, was Apricot—belly up and sound asleep. The kitten was so sweet. She didn't know how she'd ever leave her behind.

"Seems as if she couldn't be happier." He

turned back to Jules. "You're really good with her. Someday you'll make a great mother."

"It's not going to happen."

She waited, but he didn't say anything else on the matter.

Deep inside she wanted to believe him. She wanted to believe that she could someday be a mom. Lizzie wasn't the only one who'd dreamed of having her own family. But knowing she wasn't cut out to raise children, Jules had turned her focus to social work. She thought she could care for the kids from a distance. Until she'd found out that she was unable to maintain a professional distance. Frustration knotted her stomach.

Stefano made himself comfortable on the floor and started to gather a stack of papers. "So how do you do this?"

"You really want to make a flower?" She surely hadn't heard him correctly. There was nothing about this jean-clad, muscle-bound businessman that said he had a crafty bone in his body.

"Of course I do. I told you that I would do everything I could to help with this wedding. Speaking of which, I ordered those wedding favors."

"You did?"

He nodded. "You wouldn't believe all of the party favors they offer. I hope you don't mind, but I ordered a few other things. Of course, you get final approval."

Impressed with his new attitude toward the wedding, she sat down next to him. "Thank you. I can't wait to see them."

She went on to instruct him about making flowers by taking eight sheets of tissue paper and aligning them with the round paper cutter. For a while she gave him her undivided attention, but he was a quick learner. His flower wasn't perfect, but it impressed her—he impressed her. It wasn't just his flair for crafts, but his ability to put aside his misgivings about the wedding for his brother's happiness.

"Not exactly like your flowers," he said, surveying his rather limp effort.

"But not bad for your first try." She gave him some pointers, and he tried again.

"That's better."

"Yes, it is."

He turned to her. "Now that I have this flower stuff figured out, how about you tell me more about your decision not to have a family? I see the motherly instincts come out in you every time you gather that little bundle of fur in your hands."

But Apricot was so easy. She wasn't stressful. Jules didn't have to worry about messing her up for the rest of her life.

Jules punched another set of papers. "You don't want to hear this."

"Yes, I do. If you'll tell me." He sat there holding a stack of deep purple papers in his hand, staring at her with such compassion in his eyes.

What did it matter now if she told him the bitter truth? He knew the answers already; he just hadn't put it all together. But delving into those deep, dark memories made her heart pinch. It was a subject that she didn't share with anyone. She'd learned how to push those painful memories to the far recesses of her mind.

So why did she feel the temptation to open up to Stefano? Why did she want him to understand her?

"It's okay." His voice was gentle and filled with understanding. "If it's too painful, you don't have to say anything. I won't mention it again."

He was letting her off the hook just like that, with no probing questions about her scars—no judgments. Stefano was a complex man. She had the feeling he had his own ghosts hanging in the closet.

Maybe he would understand her story.

Her mouth grew dry as she struggled to swallow. "My mother, she…she tried her best. But she was a very unhappy soul. When I was little, my father left us. She did her best to find work, but without much education, her choices were limited and minimum wage doesn't pay for much. It was a tough life, and she took her frustrations out on me."

The memories of her childhood came to her in snippets. Flashes of her mother crying. The sense of insecurity. Her stomach growling when she went to bed. Over the years, Jules had tried to forget the details, but some refused to fade away.

Still she'd promised herself that she wouldn't end up like her mother. She wouldn't trust her future to a man, only to have him pull the rug out from under her. She wouldn't take her anger and frustration out on her child. And she wouldn't just quit on life.

"I'd been removed from my mother's care a few times. But I was always returned. Each time she promised that she'd get it right. But the last time..." Her voice drifted away as those dark memories resurfaced. "The last time she did this to me." Jules pointed to her scars.

She couldn't say any more. She didn't want to dissolve into a tearful mess. Perhaps she'd kept the memories locked up for too long. Stefano's presence had her letting down her defenses, leaving her vulnerable to the pain she'd neatly tucked away in the back of her heart.

She swallowed down the lump of emotions. "We should get these flowers done."

Before she could reach for the papers, Stefano

moved to her side. His hands reached out, cupping her shoulders. "I'm so sorry that happened to you. No child should ever go through what you did."

She glanced away, not wanting to see the sympathy in his eyes. "It was a long time ago."

"But it still hurts. I know."

Their gazes collided, sending her heart beating out of control. "You truly get it, don't you?"

He nodded. "We didn't have the same sort of childhood, but I know what it's like to lose a parent and hope they'll come back. And I know what it's like to be forgotten by a parent."

In that moment, she knew that she'd found someone else besides Lizzie who understood her and didn't judge her by her past. The breath hitched in her throat as her focus slipped to his mouth—his very kissable mouth. She wondered what it'd be like to be held in his strong arms and to have his lips press to hers. Would his kiss be swift and passionate? Or would it be slow and tantalizing?

She didn't have to wonder any longer as he pulled her close. Her hands grabbed hold of his broad shoulders to steady herself. When his head dipped toward her, her eyelids fluttered closed.

Her heart beat so loudly that it was all she could hear. Could Stefano hear it, too? Did he know how much she wanted him?

And then he was there, pressing his lips to hers. The hunger and need in his kiss answered her questions. He wanted her as much as she wanted him.

He tasted of coffee. Caffeine might provide a jolt of energy, but it didn't compare with the rush of adrenaline from Stefano's kiss. A moan swelled in her throat. His touch was so much better than anything she'd conjured up in her imagination.

But this wasn't right. Getting involved with Stefano would only complicate things. She had to stop before it went any further.

With every bit of willpower she could muster, she pressed her palms to his solid chest. The *thump-thump* of his heart vibrated through her fingers. Ignoring the delicious sensations that zinged up her arms, she pushed him away.

She looked at him, finding bewilderment in his eyes. Perhaps he, too, was caught off guard by the intensity of that amazing kiss.

"I…I should be going." Stefano jumped to his feet.

He beat a path through the colorful paper to the door without even a glance back. Why was he acting as though he couldn't get away from her fast enough? Was she the only one to feel anything? No, she was certain that he'd felt it, too. Then she realized that it must have unnerved him, as well.

Just then Apricot stood up, stretched and gave off a little baby *murr*. She strolled across the bed to where Jules was leaning against it and rubbed her head against Jules's hair, which was drying into an unruly mess of spiral curls.

Maybe opening up to him hadn't been the wisest move. She'd have to be careful going forward and keep a safe distance. Because his kiss was much too tempting, and she might just forget that she wasn't interested in starting up anything with him.

CHAPTER ELEVEN

"WHAT DO YOU MEAN, Lizzie canceled?"

Stefano's irritated tone echoed through the car, catching Jules's full attention.

She turned in her seat, noticing the distinct frown lines marring his face as he skillfully maneuvered them through the busy streets of Rome. Why in the world was he so upset about Lizzie's change of plans? Or was something else bothering him? Something to do with the kiss that neither dared to mention?

It didn't matter. She refused to let Lizzie's call or Stefano's gloomy mood ruin this day. This was the very best part of planning a wedding—picking out the cake.

"Lizzie mentioned that there is a special party in the dining room tonight and it's all hands on deck. You should be happy. Your grandfather's restaurant is thriving again."

"I am." Stefano sighed as he slowed to a stop

for a red light. "I'll find a place to turn around and we'll head back to the vineyard."

"Why would we do that?"

"Why not? The only reason we were heading into the city was to help the bride pick out a cake."

"And that's exactly what we're going to do."

"What?" He chanced a quick glance her way. "You've got to be kidding, right?"

"No. I'm quite serious."

He'd barely spoken to her since they'd kissed two days ago. Was it because she'd pushed him away? Or was it something more? Maybe he wasn't over the loss of his wife. Jules had spied a snapshot of him and his wife in a collage in Massimo's room. When she'd mentioned the particular photo, Massimo would only say that Gianna had died a couple of years ago. It made Jules wonder if there was more to the story—more behind Stefano's hesitation to let himself live again.

From the photo, she gathered that Stefano's wife had been nothing like her. Or perhaps it'd be better to say that Jules was nothing like his wife. Gianna had worn her long hair pulled back into a conservative braid, her face had been devoid of makeup and her clothes were quite modest and not the least bit showy. She was the quintessential wholesome, modest wife—something Jules would never be.

For the first time ever, Jules wanted to change. She wanted to be the woman who could make a simple dress look amazing. She wanted to be comfortable in her own skin and not feel the need to hide behind a wall of makeup. But more than anything she wanted a man to look at her with love and desire like Stefano had been looking at his wife in the photo. Correction: she wanted Stefano to look at her that way. But that was never going to happen.

Now he barely glanced her way—not since she'd lost her head and let things go too far. She missed the friendship they'd been building. If only she could undo that moment.

She couldn't let that stand between them doing their duty as maid of honor and best man. She was a grown-up, and so was he. They could move past this. Somehow.

She swallowed her uneasiness and hoped her voice would sound more confident than she felt inside. "We promised to do everything we could to make this wedding a success. Can you still do that?"

"But it's their wedding, not ours."

Jules's mouth opened but nothing came out. Him mentioning them and a wedding all in the same sentence caught her off guard. She wondered if it was unintentional, or if his thoughts had been straying back to the brief but heated kiss they'd shared.

His knuckles gleamed white as he gripped the steering wheel. "You know what I mean." His body visibly stiffened. "Not that you and I are getting married—I mean not that we're even involved—"

"It's okay. I know what you mean." She watched as the tension eased out of his shoulders. "But that doesn't change things. We still have to do this for Lizzie and Dante."

"I sure hope you know what you're doing."

"Trust me. I do." She grabbed her wedding planner from her purse and perused the photos of cakes that Lizzie preferred. "I know what she likes. Trust me."

"You keep saying that, but I just don't know."

"If it makes you feel any better, Lizzie picked out photos of cakes. We weren't sure what the baker could produce on such short notice, so I had her line up her choices in order of what she liked best." Jules flipped to the section where she'd taped the pictures of the cakes. "None of these look too elaborate."

"If you say so. Now where exactly am I supposed to be going?"

She read off the directions to the first bakery. While he navigated the congested roadway, she settled back in the comfortable leather seat and thumbed through her organizer. There was still so much to do for this quickly approaching wedding, but it was her escort that kept distracting her. The memory of his kiss was always lurking at the edge of her thoughts. Why couldn't she forget it? Why did this one have to stand out in her mind?

Going forward, she had to be careful not to let it happen again. These DeFiore men came armed with irresistible smiles, alluring dark eyes that drew you in, and when they talked to you, it was as if you were the only person that existed. Lizzie had already fallen hook, line and sinker. But Jules was smarter than that. She wasn't going to let her heart do the thinking for her. She knew too well that the L word wasn't enough.

Her father had told her that he loved her and that he was doing what was best for her. Then he'd left. She never saw him again. It wasn't until she was a teenager that she learned he'd died in an auto accident. Then there was her mother, who would tell her that she loved her, but when times got tough, her temper would flare and she'd turn to alcohol.

If that was love, she didn't want any part of it. Growing up, Jules and Lizzie never talked about love. They both quietly acknowledged that they cherished each other like sisters but neither could bring themselves to say the L word. It was as if vocalizing the emotion would jinx their entire relationship. Jules had since avoided the word altogether.

Jules was grateful for the distraction as they pulled up to Sweet Things Bakery. Her anticipation was short-lived—they were booked. Soon they found that Spagnoli's Bakery, Antonio's Bake Shop and Cake Haven were also booked. Weddings were a big business. And it was first come, first served.

"This isn't looking too good." Stefano started the car.

"Thank you, Captain Obvious."

He glanced at her with surprise written all over his face. And then, instead of grouching at her, he started to laugh. And laugh. To be honest, she didn't know what there was to laugh about. How in the world were they supposed to have a wedding without a cake?

Stefano gathered himself. "So how are you at baking?"

"You've got to be kidding." He was kidding, wasn't he? She looked him in the eyes and saw a glint of seriousness. "I'm awful. I can't even make a box cake, not without it falling. My baking skills are not pretty at all. We have to find a bakery to do the wedding cake, even if it means visiting every single bakery in this city."

When they pulled up in front of Tortino

Paradiso—Cupcake Heaven—Jules knew they were in the right place. It may not be the wedding cake that Lizzie was dreaming of. But in times of desperation, there had to be compromises.

The building was a dark-chocolate brick. The striped awning was the color of pink-and-pearl-white frosting. And the large windows held various cupcake towers as well as cupcakes displayed in the shape of a smiley face. The display that truly caught Jules's attention was one of cupcakes decorated as various brightly colored flowers and placed in a garden setting with a white picket fence. It was detailed, imaginative and fun. The bakery radiated a sense of cheerful creativity where the sky was the limit.

"This is it!"

Stefano turned a puzzled look her way. "This is what?"

"This is the place where we'll find Lizzie and Dante's cake."

"Maybe your Italian isn't so good. This is a cupcake shop. I don't think that's what they had in mind for their wedding cake."

"Just trust me."

"That's what I'm afraid of."

She jumped out of the car before Stefano could say more. She pulled off her sunglasses and smiled at a customer who'd just exited the bakery. In their hand was a cute bag with the picture of a chocolate cupcake with pink frosting on the front. It appeared that this place was all about the details. Now they had to pass one last test—the taste test.

Stefano rounded the car and joined her on the sidewalk. She leaned toward him and whispered, "Just follow my lead. Or else."

Without waiting for his response, she reached out and slid her hand in his. Goose bumps raced up her arm, and a warm sensation swirled in her chest. She resisted the urge to glance his way to see if he noticed her reaction to his touch. She willed herself to breath regularly and act nonchalant. She assured herself that the reaction had nothing to do with that much-too-short kiss.

"Is this really necessary?" He glanced down at their clasped hands, but he didn't pull away.

"Most definitely." She swallowed the lump in her throat. "I'm not about to let this place slip through our fingers. So to speak."

"Shouldn't you call Lizzie and let her know what you have in mind?"

"I will."

"When?"

"When I know that this place can fit the wedding on their calendar. Otherwise there's no point in consulting Lizzie. She may not be here, but she's still the bride and brides do get nervous.

If she knew how many bakeries had turned us away, she'd start to panic. Is that what you want?"

"No, but—"

"That's what I thought. Now let's get moving. The only way to find out anything is to ask."

They walked up to the bakery hand in hand. Jules hoped that she looked more confident than she felt. It bothered her that the only way he'd hold her hand was by way of a threat. He probably would rather do a hundred other less desirable things than act as if they were a happy couple. But he was doing his best to be a good brother and keep his word to Dante—not many people would go to this length.

Like the gentleman she knew him to be, Stefano opened the glass door for her. When she passed by him, she caught a hint of his spicy cologne. She'd never been one to pay much attention to those sorts of things, but in Stefano's case, she found the inviting scent quite appealing. In fact, she was quite tempted to pause and get a much better whiff.

The chime above the door startled her from her daydream. What was she thinking? She wasn't in Italy to get involved with a man, casually or otherwise. Her lips pressed firmly together as she held back a frustrated sigh. When the store clerk spotted them, it was with great effort that Jules forced her mouth into a smile.

"Showtime," she whispered to Stefano. "Remember this is for your brother and my sister." She didn't know if the warning was more for him or her.

"Hi," the saleswoman with a pink-and-brown-striped apron said from behind the counter. "If there's anything I can do to help you, just let me know."

"Actually, there is something." Jules led the way to the counter. "We want to know if you have an opening for a July wedding."

"Let me just pull up my calendar." The woman had a friendly smile and a bouncy ponytail. She typed in the information. "Any particular date?"

Jules read off the date as the woman's fingers clicked over the keyboard. Then an ominous silence came over the showroom. Jules's chest tightened as she waited for the verdict. The woman said nothing, and then she typed a little more. Behind her dark-rimmed glasses, her eyes narrowed and her forehead creased.

"This summer is so busy. It seems like everyone is getting married."

Jules wanted to press her for an answer, but she used every bit of willpower not to sound overbearing and pushy. "Yes, it's a great summer for a wedding."

Was that a sigh she heard from Stefano? She glanced his way, but he was still wearing that stoic expression as he pretended to be totally absorbed in the array of cupcakes in the display case.

The silence was unnerving. If this place couldn't help them, she didn't know what they were going to do. Chances were really good that at this late date every bakery was booked. Lizzie would be crushed. After waiting all this time to find her soul mate, this wedding had to go on without a hitch—or at least go on.

"We'll take anything you can do." Jules didn't care at this point if she sounded desperate. She was desperate.

When Stefano flexed his fingers, she realized that she had a death grip on him. She loosened her hold and lifted onto her tiptoes to peer over the counter, but she was at the wrong angle to read the computer monitor.

The woman glanced over at her. "I know you're anxious for an answer, but I have a bit of a conflict. I'm checking to see if there is a way around it. If you just give me one more minute."

"Sure. Whatever it takes. I know this is short notice, but it's so important."

The saleswoman smiled. "I understand. You two are a cute couple."

Jules felt Stefano's gaze on her. He wanted her to correct the woman, and she would, just not yet.

They needed a spot on the calendar before Jules would risk rocking the boat.

"Okay, I can make this work. It just took a bit of juggling."

Jules released Stefano's hand and clapped her hands together. She was more wound up about this than she'd realized.

"If you could just give me your name, I'll add you to the calendar."

Jules supplied the necessary information. The last part that might mess up this arrangement was the location of the wedding. She hesitantly informed her that the wedding and reception would be outside the city at the vineyard, but the woman barely batted an eye except to tell her that there'd be an additional delivery fee. Jules told her that would be perfectly fine.

They now had dresses, flowers and a cake, of sorts. This wedding was going to come together. And Jules had already figured out what to do about the food. Dante's family had been anxious to help; they could do covered dishes. From what she'd learned in her short time in Rome, the De-Fiore family was a group of accomplished cooks. She couldn't imagine buying anything that tasted anywhere as good as the dishes they made in the restaurant.

Right now was Jules's favorite part of the wedding preparations—a chance to sample mouthwatering cakes from dark chocolate to angelic white. Or in this case, sample the wide array of cupcakes. Jules grinned like a little kid as she eyed the display case filled with cupcakes decorated in every imaginable color.

"Relax." The woman smiled at Stefano. "I promise this won't hurt at all. In fact, you might enjoy it. If you two would just have a seat at the table over there, I'll grab some samples."

"Thank you." Jules took Stefano's hand and led him to the table. Once they were seated, Jules turned to him. "Would you relax? You're making everyone uncomfortable."

"What?" Stefano glanced across the little white café-style table at her.

"Cheer up. This won't take long, and you get to taste some delicious cupcakes."

"Sorry. I was thinking about something else."

"I'm sure you were," she mumbled.

"I was." His gaze narrowed in on her. "I was thinking about the vineyard."

Apparently she hadn't spoken quite as softly as she'd thought. "Are you that bored that you'd rather be working?"

"Why must you jump to conclusions?"

She shrugged. Was she wrong? Was it possible he wasn't wishing he was anywhere but here with her?

"Then why were you thinking about the vineyard?"

He leaned the little chair back on its two rear legs and crossed his arms as though trying to decide if he should take her into his confidence. That bothered her. After everything she'd told him about her past, he really had to decide if she was trustworthy?

Before she could say a word, he spoke up. "It was brought to my attention that I've been cutting my father out of the business side of things at the vineyard. I guess I was so intent on keeping busy after Gianna died that I hadn't noticed that he felt cut out. That was never my intention."

"And you think your father wants more responsibility."

Stefano nodded. "He's succeeded in keeping everything under control while I've been helping you with the wedding. And he seems happier. But then again, I don't know if it's the winery or if he's falling in love."

"What? With whom?"

Before Stefano could answer, the saleswoman returned with a tray full of cupcakes. Jules's mouth started to water just looking at the beautiful little cakes. With a knife they cut the cupcakes in half. The flavors ranged from lemon with buttercream frosting to red velvet with cream cheese frosting to banana crème. All in all there were eight flavors to choose from.

Jules didn't know how she was going to make such a truly difficult decision. All of them tasted divine except maybe the vanilla. It was good, but in comparison to the others, it was a bit boring.

"Well, did you make a decision?" the woman asked after returning from helping some other customers.

"I don't know. They're all so good." Needing some help, she turned to Stefano. "What do you think?"

She didn't normally turn to a man for advice. Typically the men she'd dated never wanted to involve themselves in decision making of any form. It was easier to stand on the sidelines and let someone else do the problem solving. And she wouldn't bother asking for Stefano's input, but this decision was a big one. She didn't want to get it wrong.

Who was she trying to kid? She valued Stefano's opinion a lot. He had good taste and…she liked him. Even though he wasn't crazy about weddings, he'd turned his life upside down to help her out. Someday when he was ready to get on with his life, he'd make somebody a good husband.

She glanced across the table at him. He smiled

at her, and her heart gave off a fluttering sensation. What were they talking about?

His gaze moved to the tray, now littered with crumbs. "I think I like the espresso with buttercream."

"You do? Really?" He was a man after her own tastes. When he nodded to confirm his choice, she countered with, "But what if not everyone cares for coffee flavor?"

The young woman spoke up. "That's not a problem. You know that we can do two flavors."

"That would be great." Since he'd stepped up and picked out one flavor, now it was her turn. "I think the other should be strawberry with the cream cheese."

The woman started typing in the information. She paused and looked at Stefano. "And the groom's name?"

Jules wasn't about to let him mess this up. "The thing is he isn't exactly the groom."

"Really?" The woman's brows rose beneath her bangs. "But you two look so perfect together. I would have sworn—oh, never mind. It's none of my business. If you'll just tell me your groom's name, I'll put it in the computer."

She didn't want the woman to get the wrong idea. "I'm not the bride. We—" Jules pointed back and forth between her and Stefano "—are the maid of honor and the best man."

The woman's eyes lit up and the worry lines left her face. "That makes sense, because I could sense that you two are a couple. And quite in love with each other. I can always tell these things."

Stefano leaned forward and opened his mouth. Before he could utter a single syllable, Jules kicked him under the table. His mouth snapped shut, and his brows drew together as he glared at her. She smiled broadly back at him, hoping to soothe his ruffled feathers.

"Now that we have that straightened out, if you'll just give me the name of the bride and the groom, we'll get this order in the system."

When they finally walked out the door, Jules was amazed at how laid-back and easygoing the woman was about the wedding. She had actually been sympathetic about Lizzie having to work instead of getting the chance to do the actual planning of her wedding.

Now if only everything else would fall into place. And Jules didn't just mean for the wedding. No, she had something else in mind. A chance for people to see her as something more than a scarred-up goth chick.

But to do that, she'd have to let her guard down. She'd have to do away with the things that after all these years were inherently her. Could she do it? And would it make a difference to Stefano?

CHAPTER TWELVE

WHAT WAS UP with Jules?

More importantly, what was up with him?

Stefano stared blindly at the blinking cursor on the computer monitor. Ever since they'd kissed, things had shifted between them. He'd lost his footing where Jules was concerned. And try as he might to get back to that solid ground of casual acquaintances, he couldn't quite reach that plateau.

Instead, he'd tried losing himself in his work, like he'd done ever since Gianna's tragic death, but that wasn't working, either. His father was quite productive. By the time Stefano got back from his excursions to Rome with Jules, there wasn't much for him to do, certainly nothing comprehensive requiring his full attention. And time on his hands at this point was not a good thing. All he could think about was kissing Jules. A definite no-no.

Resisting her was getting harder and harder,

especially when she slipped her soft hand in his. Did she have any clue what her touch did to him? And then she'd lift her chin and smile up at him, and his heart would career into his ribs. His common sense fizzled and shorted out. His only saving grace had been that she always pulled away before he could act on his impulses.

With a frustrated sigh, he glanced at the clock, finding it was almost lunchtime. He shut down the computer. It'd been a waste of a morning as he'd barely gotten a thing done for thinking about his beautiful houseguest.

Yesterday after they'd left the bakery, Jules had wanted some time to do a little shopping. He hadn't minded. He'd needed some time alone before sharing the small confines of the auto with her. He especially needed a break after that lady at the bakery kept going on and on about them being a couple. And it didn't help that sometimes when Jules turned her green gaze on him, it was as though she was trying to tell him something— as if she wanted more from him than what he could offer her...or anyone.

Or was he seeing what he wanted to see? That thought stopped him in his tracks as he made his way from the barn to the house. Was it possible Jules, with her outrageous makeup and hip clothes, had somehow gotten to him? His steps faltered. After all this time telling himself that he'd had it with love, was he starting to fall for the girl from New York?

He gave his head a shake. Wasn't going to happen. He resumed his trek to the villa. Suddenly his appetite for lunch had disappeared. All he could think about was Jules and how her green eyes spoke to him—telling him of her past emotional wounds. His gut reaction was to protect her and show her that life didn't have to be so hard. But how could he do that when he knew for a fact that life was unpredictable and quite unfair?

No, the best thing he could do for both of them was to back away. He'd been wrong to get so invested in this wedding. He might be the groom's brother and best man, but he didn't do wedding planning. By now Jules should know how to get into the city on her own and with all the electronic wizardry on her phone, she'd find her way around.

Yes, that's what he'd do. He'd back out of this wedding froufrou and submerge himself in work. After all, there was a tour and wine-tasting event on the calendar. He could think of ways to expand it, perhaps by adding some tales from his family's colorful history. He didn't have anything specific in mind, but he'd think on it.

He'd just neared the house when Jules stepped outside. His thoughts screeched to a halt as he took in her appearance. Her very different appearance. He blinked to make sure he wasn't seeing things.

She was wearing a pale blue cotton dress. It was short, just above the knee, and the skirt flared out a bit. The waist was snug and hinted at her curves. Her very fine curves. He struggled to keep his mouth from gaping open. His gaze traveled up over the white stripes of the bodice and stopped at her bare shoulders and arms. The only things holding up that scrap of a dress were two thin straps. A lump formed in his throat.

She smiled at him, and the whole world seemed to glow. "Do you like my new purchase?"

"It's um…very nice." He forced his gaze to meet hers.

"Walk with me."

Her request wasn't a question, but rather a honeyed command—one he wasn't about to disobey. She passed by him, and all he could do was stare. It was then that he noticed her hair. There were no ponytails. Instead her dark wavy hair was loose and flowing down her back. *What in the world?* She'd never worn it like that before, but he certainly approved.

He took long strides to catch up to her. "Where are we going?"

"To the barn. I still haven't seen it, and I thought…well, I hoped that you might have a few minutes to show me around."

She wanted to see the winery? And she wanted him to show her around? What could it hurt? Maybe this would be a good prelude to him letting her know that he'd changed his mind about working on the wedding planning with her.

"Sure. Is there anything in particular that you want to see?"

Her sun-kissed shoulders rose and fell. "Whatever you want to show me will be fine."

She was actually interested in his work—in his heritage. That was an area where Gianna had never showed any interest. The only thing that she had to say about the vineyard was that it took up all his time and that it kept them from moving to the city. He hadn't realized when they'd married that she expected a different sort of life. He figured that marrying a local girl would ensure that they both wanted a quiet way of life. He'd been so wrong.

He gave Jules the grand tour, starting at the office, and then they moved on to the processing room, where during the harvest the grapes were hand sorted. He showed her the barrel room where the wine was aged. The tour concluded in the spacious wine-tasting room with its long, thin table for the guests.

"We should head back for lunch." He guided her outside.

"Thank you for the personal tour. I really enjoyed it. I'm just sorry I'll miss seeing all of the activity during the harvest."

"You always have an open invitation to return anytime."

She peered deeply into his eyes, and his heart thumped hard and fast. When she glanced away, her butterfly tattoo caught his attention. Just the tips of the wings peeked out of the dress's neckline. He longed to see all of it. He'd never seen anything so captivating. A struggle warred within him—common sense versus his raging testosterone. And the testosterone was taking the lead.

Jules turned away and started to walk. "This estate is so big. You certainly don't have to worry about bothering any of your neighbors."

The land was the last thing on his mind, but he struggled to make intelligent conversation. "Over the generations, it has grown. Buying more of the surrounding properties was a priority."

"Are you still looking into expanding?"

"If the opportunity presents itself, sure. But it isn't my focus." His only interest now was finding out if her lips were as sweet as the finest brachetto grape.

"What is your priority?"

It was on the tip of his tongue to say that it was her—that making her deliriously happy was his priority. But he bit back the ridiculous words before he could utter them. What in the world was getting into him?

He cleared his throat as he searched for a reasonable answer. "The quality of the wine. And broadening our interaction with the public."

Her footsteps were muffled by the grass. "Sounds exciting."

"You think so?"

"I do. I love the vineyard. I'm sure others will love it, too. It's so peaceful and relaxing. I can see why you stayed on and continue to work with your father."

"But surely you wouldn't do the same thing if roles were reversed." She was a city girl, born and bred. The tranquility was just a novelty thing. Sooner or later she'd want to move on…just like his late wife.

"I could definitely see me living here. In another world, I'd have a big family with lots of room for the kids to play. And cats. And dogs. And maybe a horse or two."

"Talk about a menagerie. Are you sure you'd be up for all of that?"

She shrugged. "It isn't like it's ever going to happen. I don't live here, and as you well know I'm not exactly the poster girl for motherhood. But sometimes it's nice to dream."

"I don't see why you have to dream when you can make it a reality. Well, at least the part of being a mother and having a menagerie of cats and dogs."

She stopped and stared up at him. "Look at me."

He did as she asked. His heart started to pound again. He held his body rigid, resisting the urge to pull her close. He recalled vividly how soft her curves were, and his resolve wavered.

"No, really look at me." Her serious tone snapped him to attention. "What do you see?"

"I see your beautiful face without all of that makeup."

"I didn't see much point in it without air-conditioning. I end up wiping most of it off throughout the day."

"That's good." When her brows lifted in a questioning fashion, he added, "I mean it's good that you gave up on the makeup. You don't need it."

The truth was that she was even more beautiful without it. She had such a fresh young face, and it needed no enhancement at all. He was captivated by her natural beauty. And with her hair loose and blowing in the breeze, she had a down-to-earth appeal. No longer did she look like she'd just walked off a rock video. Now she looked like someone who might actually belong in his world. But part of him missed her hip, chic look. That in and of itself surprised him.

Her head tilted to the side, but her gaze never left his. "What are you thinking?"

He hadn't realized he'd gotten so caught up in his thoughts. "I was thinking about you."

"And what did you decide?"

"That you are beautiful." He looked deep into her eyes and saw disbelief. He'd have to prove it to her. "Your green eyes are a shade or two deeper than the grape leaves. And your long, dark lashes make your eyes very alluring. Your skin is smooth and makes me long to run my fingers down its velvety softness."

Color rose in her cheeks. "You're missing the point. The scars. You can't miss them. And they're ugly."

"They aren't ugly. You aren't ugly."

She shook her head. "You're just saying that to make me feel better."

"I'm speaking the truth." He desperately wanted her to believe him.

"No, you aren't." She let out an exasperated sigh. "I didn't tell you the details before, maybe I should now. Maybe then you'll understand why I find the scars so ugly."

He opened his mouth to protest but then closed it without saying a word. Perhaps talking about it would be good for her.

"I told you that my mother did this to me, but what I didn't tell you was that it was during one of her drunken bouts. She was angry because she'd run out of vodka. I was on my way home from playing with the neighbor. She smacked me and I lost my balance at the top of the porch steps. Down I went, hitting…hitting my head on the edge of the steps and landing on the cement sidewalk."

Stefano clenched his hands. How could a mother do that to her own child? It was inconceivable. And yet the only words he could find to convey his sympathy seemed so inadequate. And it really didn't matter because no words could make up for what she'd experienced at the hand of the one person who was supposed to love and protect her.

"I'm so sorry."

"Don't be. It was the best thing to happen to me." Her eyes were shiny with unshed tears, but she kept it together. "When I lived with my mother, there was never enough to eat. Rarely was there clean laundry. And the longer it went on, the meaner she became. If they hadn't taken me away, I'd have never met Lizzie." Jules stopped and drew in an uneven breath. "My mother wasn't strong enough to take care of both of us. Eventually she turned to drugs and OD'd. Now do you finally understand why I shouldn't be a mother?"

"I think that you're amazing and the strongest person I know." He meant every single word. She had impressed him before this, and now he was just in awe of her. "And above it all, I still believe you can achieve whatever you set your mind on. But none of that changes what I see when I look at you. You're beautiful. From the wrinkle in your forehead when you're confused to the tip of your nose to your rosy lips that are just ripe for tasting."

And without thinking of the ramifications of what he was about to do, he leaned forward and lowered his head. The only thing that mattered now was making her feel better. He had to let her know that those scars didn't define her. She was beautiful in spite of them. And her beauty resonated from the inside out.

His lips gently brushed against hers. He didn't want to scare her off. When he pulled back a little, he heard her undeniable sigh of enjoyment. She liked his touch, and he liked touching her. What would it hurt to follow up that kiss with another one?

He sought out her lips again. They were sweet like chocolate. His hands slipped around her waist, and she leaned into him. He'd been waiting so long to do this again. And it was even better than what he'd remembered.

The kiss went on and on. She should be kissed like this and often. Jules deserved to be cherished and loved. And if somehow he could convince her of this, he would. He couldn't imagine her throwing her life away because of some scars that weren't even that noticeable.

Her soft curves molded perfectly to him. And when a soft moan reached his ears, he wasn't so sure which of them had made the sound of pure pleasure. Not that it mattered as her fingers wrapped around his neck and raked through his hair, sending a whole new wave of excitement through him. Every nerve ending stood at attention.

"Beautiful day, isn't it?"

The sound of his father's distant voice sent them flying apart as though lightning had struck the ground between them. Her cheeks turned a dusty pink and her lips a shade of deep rosy red. She looked as if she'd been ravished. And he'd never seen her look more beautiful.

Stefano gave himself a mental jerk. What in the world had he just let happen? His gaze sought out Jules. He meant to send her a sympathetic look, but her eyes wouldn't meet his. Instead of making things better, he'd only succeeded in making them worse.

Him, the man who'd sworn off relationships, was standing in the open, drowning in the sweetest kiss. Not that the kiss constituted a relationship. He combed his fingers through his hair. Somehow he had to put things back on track between them. He promised himself that he wouldn't lose control around her again.

With his father just far enough down the path, Stefano lowered his voice to say, "That shouldn't have happened. I don't know what I was thinking. It…it was a mistake. I know neither of us is looking for a relationship."

He steeled himself and turned to his father, who was making his way to the house from the winery. His father's eyes danced with merriment, but his face was devoid of the mischievous smile that Stefano could only imagine would materialize after he passed them.

"I…we were just on our way back from a tour of the winery."

His father nodded. "I guess I don't need to ask how it went."

Stefano couldn't believe he was having such fun at his expense. This was something his father never would have bothered with when he was a kid. Back then his father was quite stoic and didn't joke around. But lately he'd been seeing more and more changes in him. Any other time Stefano would have welcomed this transformation, but not now—not with Jules. And not when he'd made such a monumental mistake. Whatever made him think that kissing her was such a good idea?

"Stefano, did you hear me?"

His father was staring at him expectantly, but Stefano hadn't heard a word. "What?"

"I said you better hurry or you'll never catch up to her."

Stefano glanced around, finding that Jules had taken off toward the house. *Great!* Could this get any worse? He stopped that line of thought as he knew all too well that things could always get worse. He swore under his breath.

He started after her. He didn't have a clue what he would say to her. Maybe it'd be best to just let her go. She'd get over the kiss quickly enough. After all, it hadn't meant anything. Nothing at all. Except it felt as if it had been the beginning of something—something profound. His teeth ground together as he stifled a groan of frustration.

His world had been orderly until Jules had entered it. He was a widower of his own making. Being alone was punishment for his actions. If he hadn't been so stubborn, if he hadn't pushed Gianna into marrying him, she'd still be here—still be alive. His footsteps faltered.

The problems came after they'd married and he'd found out that they wanted different things in life. She wanted excitement and fun. He wanted stability and routine. Where he enjoyed kicking back in front of the large-screen television to watch football, she wanted to dress up and go to the theater. The love they'd initially felt started to dwindle with each passionate disagreement. And then that fateful night.

He couldn't let the past repeat itself. Though he highly doubted that Jules would take off in his car, he couldn't take the chance. He couldn't let this misunderstanding linger between them. There had to be a way to fix what he'd broken. Maybe if he'd have done that with Gianna, she'd still be alive.

When he entered the kitchen, Jules was nowhere to be found. Maria stood at the counter, stirring a pasta salad. She turned to him. It wasn't often just the two of them stood in the kitchen. He was tempted to ask her if there was something going on between her and his father. He resisted, still unsure how he felt about the idea of them hooking up.

"Did you need something?" Maria wiped her hands on a little white apron trimmed with purple grapes.

"Um, no." Now wasn't the time to get into it. He had enough problems on his hands.

"Are you sure? Because if you're looking for Jules, she tore through here a minute or two ago." Maria sent him a disapproving look before pointing to the upstairs.

"Thanks. I'll check on her." He rushed past Maria and headed for the spiraling staircase. He took the steps two at a time. He didn't know what he'd say to Jules when he found her. He'd have to wing this one.

What a fool she'd been.

Jules picked up Apricot and snuggled her nose down into the downy soft fur. A loud purr vibrated through the little kitten's body. Tears stung the back of her eyes, but she refused to let them fall.

What had she been thinking back there in the field? It was as if she were a kid with the biggest crush in the world. When Stefano had looked at her with desire in his eyes, she'd forgotten everything but feeling the excitement and passion of his lips moving over hers.

Then to have him push away from her and try to dismiss the moment as though it meant nothing hurt more than the rude comments she'd received back in school about her scars. The cruel comments kids threw out about how she was defective and that's why her own parents didn't even want her had cut deeply. But Stefano's actions had surpassed that pain.

Why, oh, why did she ever think that he might be different? Just because his brother had accepted Lizzie with her less-than-stellar past didn't mean that Stefano would be as open-minded. Sure he said all the right things, but that was just because he was a gentleman. It didn't mean that everything he said was true—not when it came to her scars or her past.

A knock at her door had Apricot squirming to get out of her hands. Jules moved next to the bed so that the little one would have a soft landing.

"Who is it?"

"It's Stefano. We need to talk."

"No, we don't." She was being childish, and she knew it. She just didn't know what to say to him at the moment. Her emotions were raw and conflicting.

"I hope you're decent because I'm coming in."

She started for the door, but before she could get to it, it swung open. And there stood Stefano. His large physique filled the doorway. There was no getting past him even if she wanted to. His forehead was creased, and his dark brows were drawn together. His gaze zeroed in on her and made her want to turn away, but she refused to let on how much he'd hurt her.

She leveled her shoulders and crossed her arms. "What do you want?"

"I told you we need to talk."

"And I told you I don't want to talk. I…I have stuff to do."

"Such as?"

"I need to make more paper flowers." Deciding that it would be good to have something to do with her hands, she moved to the dresser and started gathering the items she'd need.

She heard the door swing shut, followed by his approaching footsteps. His fingers encircled her arm. "Those can wait. This can't."

She glanced at his hand on her bare arm and then lifted her chin. "You make it sound like life or death."

"It could be." He sighed and shook his head. "I need to apologize."

"Wait. Why might this be life or death?" What was she missing? Obviously it was something big.

"Because…oh, it doesn't matter. I want to apologize for kissing you—"

"Why? It isn't your fault that this—" she pointed to the half-moon scar next to her eye "—is so ugly that it repulses you." She started to turn away.

He gripped her shoulders in his strong hands and pulled her around so that they were face-to-face. "It doesn't repulse me. How many times do I have to tell you that you're beautiful before you believe me?"

She shook her head, fighting back the tears that were threatening to fall. "But the scars *are* ugly. I'm ugly. That's why I wear the makeup. It hides things."

"You don't have to hide." His voice was deep and soothing.

"Yes, I do." She pulled away from his hold.

"Look at me. I tried to play this your way. I tried to look like everyone else around here. I bought different clothes. I didn't put on my makeup. I even brushed out my hair and wore it loose. And still it doesn't work. I'm still different."

He smiled at her. "You're right—you are different."

If this was his way of making her feel better, he was doing a lousy job. "Just go."

"Not until I tell you this." When she didn't look at him, his thumb moved to her chin and lifted it. "Being different isn't bad. Being different is something to be proud of. Just make sure you're doing it because it's what makes you happy and you aren't doing it just to make a statement or to hide."

"I wanted to dress like the other women in your life. I wanted to be like everyone else."

"You'll never be like everyone else. You are special. To me."

And then his head dipped and his lips pressed to hers. Her heart tumbled in her chest. He did care about her, scars and all. She knew that life wasn't that easy and that she shouldn't fall for him, but the reasons to hold back and keep him at a safe distance were eluding her at the moment.

His kiss was filled with heat, leaving no doubt in her mind that he desired her. And she wanted him, too. She wanted him more than she could say. But when he lifted his head and looked her in the eyes, the doubts started to crowd in.

"They'll be looking for us at lunch." Her feet refused to cooperate. She stayed right there in his very capable arms.

"They won't wonder about us for long."

Heat rose to her cheeks. "They know you're up here with me?"

He nodded. "Maria pointed out your whereabouts. Don't worry—no one will disturb us."

Suddenly she felt like a kid making out in her boyfriend's house with his parents in the next room. She knew she was being ridiculous. This was a massive villa. The dining room and kitchen were at the other end. And they were consenting adults. Still…

"I want you." Stefano's voice was husky with desire, leaving no doubt in her mind about his intention.

"I want you, too."

CHAPTER THIRTEEN

"WHAT'S GOING ON between you and Stefano?"

"Nothing." Jules avoided meeting Lizzie's inquisitive gaze as they sat on the living room floor of the villa. "Whatever you're thinking, just let it go."

Why did Lizzie have to pick today of all days to drive to the vineyard to help with the wedding details? Jules held back a yawn as she reached for the glue.

She didn't want to lie to Lizzie about Stefano. But she didn't know what to tell her sister because quite honestly she didn't know what was going on herself. She'd been awake most of the night replaying everything between them. How could she explain something when she didn't understand it herself?

After she and Stefano had made love, he'd kissed her goodbye and spent the rest of the day and evening at the winery. He said they were preparing for a wine-tasting event that weekend. She told herself that his absence meant nothing. That he was just taking care of his responsibilities.

But a nagging voice kept telling her that he was intentionally avoiding her. Instead of their lovemaking bringing them together, it had driven them apart. But why?

"There's something going on between you." It was on the tip of Jules's tongue to deny it when Lizzie continued, "You aren't falling for him, are you?"

Jules shook her head vehemently. "You don't have to worry. Just because you found your Prince Charming doesn't mean that I want the same thing."

Lizzie straightened and eyed her from across the coffee table. "I know that it's easy to get caught up in all of this wedding stuff and start to daydream about falling in love."

Jules stopped gluing together another fan with the wedding program printed on it. "You don't have to worry. Stefano has been nice and all, but my future isn't here—"

"You're right. I don't know what got into me. You're too smart to throw away your exciting future for anything or anyone." Lizzie's stiff posture eased. I'm just so proud of you for getting into grad school. You'll see—the time will fly by."

This was Jules's opening—a chance to tell Lizzie that she'd had a change of heart. But she'd have to do it gently. She could tell Lizzie was already nervous about the wedding. "What if I didn't go back to school?"

Lizzie's head lifted. Her focus narrowed in on Jules. A long moment of silence passed, and then Lizzie smiled. "You know, you scared me. Don't do that. For a moment, I thought that you were serious."

Jules's palms grew moist. "You make it sound like grad school is the only worthwhile option."

"It is." Lizzie leaned forward, her elbows resting on her knees. "I don't understand. I thought this is what you wanted—what we've been working toward."

"But what if I changed my mind?" She prayed Lizzie would understand. "What if I don't have what it takes to get through the program?"

"So that's what this is all about." Lizzie leaned back and sighed. "Jules, you don't have to worry. You're going to do great. You're the smartest person I know."

"I'm not that smart." Still it felt good knowing that her sister thought that highly of her.

"Smart enough to get honors in college and get accepted to your first-choice school. To me that's very impressive. Just don't stress yourself out. You can do anything you set your mind on."

"But what if—"

"Lizzie, are you ready to go?" Dante strolled

into the room, rubbing his hands together as though he was ready to hit the road.

"Yeah, I'm ready." Lizzie put her supplies in a nearby box. "Did you remember to pack the recipes your aunt gave me?"

Dante nodded. "I got them."

"And the photos your father gave me of when you were little."

"I got those, too. Mind telling me what you plan to do with all of that stuff?"

Lizzie smiled up at him, and he just shook his head. "Well, you better get moving. We have to get ready for tomorrow's filming, and I want to do some prep work tonight on the menu."

Lizzie turned to Jules. "I'm sorry I can't stay longer and help more."

"Don't worry. I've got this."

"And make sure you ask my brother for help," Dante told her as he offered Lizzie a hand to help her off the floor.

When Lizzie got to her feet, she leaned forward just as natural as could be and pressed a quick kiss to his lips. The look that passed between them spoke of their boundless love. Jules smiled. This just confirmed that all her hard work for the wedding was so worth it. This truly was her sister's happily-ever-after.

Lizzie turned back to her. "I'm taking the rest of the fans with me to finish. And I have the heavy paper for the place cards. I'll run them off on the printer in the office once we have a finalized guest list."

Jules placed the rest of the programs in the box and closed the lid. "I don't think you have to worry about that. My guess is everyone will attend. No one wants to miss the celebration."

"You don't think they're all coming because it's supposed to be filmed for television, do you?"

Dante wrapped an arm over his future wife's shoulders. "My family is all about the celebrating and it has nothing to do with television."

Lizzie gazed into Dante's eyes. "I hope you're right."

"Trust me. They're happy for us."

Lizzie reached up and squeezed his hand.

"I wouldn't trust him." Stefano stepped into the room. "If there's one thing I learned growing up with him, it is to be wary when he says 'trust me,' especially if it involves the last of the gelato."

Dante smiled and turned to his brother. "Hey, I can't help that you were so gullible."

"What did you expect me to do when you said Papa was looking for me and to trust you that there'd be some gelato left when I returned?"

"See? You learned a valuable lesson—eat your gelato first." Dante smiled broadly over the memory of outsmarting his older brother. "We've got to go."

"Don't worry." Lizzie turned back to Jules. "Everything will work out."

And with that Lizzie and Dante carried the wedding supplies out the door, leaving her alone with Stefano. He turned a puzzled face her way.

"What did she mean about everything working out?"

Jules shook her head and got to her feet. "It's nothing."

She turned her back to him and bent over, picking up her supplies. She wasn't going to get into another discussion about her education. He'd probably side with Lizzie anyhow, and she didn't need people ganging up on her. When were people going to trust her to make her own decisions?

He stepped forward and wrapped his hands around her shoulders, and turned her around to face him. "I know that something is bothering you. Did you tell her? You know, about us?"

"No. Why would you think that?"

"I don't know. Women like to confide in each other, and I thought that you might have said something."

"I wouldn't know what to say." Her frustration and insecurities came bubbling to the surface. "You and I never talked about what it meant. You've made yourself scarce since then."

He arched a brow. "You make it sound like I've been hiding from you—"

"Haven't you?" She dropped down on the couch, and he joined her.

"I've been busy. You know that."

"Uh-huh." He surely didn't think she was going to buy that he didn't have one spare moment to speak to her, did he?

"It's the truth. There's a wine-tasting event this weekend, and I've been helping my father nail down the details. But don't change the subject. We were talking about what your sister said. What's going to work out?"

Jules sighed. "I was trying to tell my sister that I'm not so sure that I still want to go to grad school."

"And..."

"And she thinks I have cold feet. She's certain I'll get over it and things will go according to plan."

"Is that how you feel?"

"No." It was the truth, and she was tired of holding it all inside.

His tone softened. "Then talk to me. Tell me what's on your mind."

Maybe Lizzie wasn't ready to hear what she was feeling, but Stefano genuinely seemed interested. And she felt as though she could confide in him. Maybe he'd surprise her and be in her corner.

"The truth is I no longer want to go to grad school."

"That's a big decision. What changed your mind?"

"Are you really interested?" She didn't want to go on and on if he was only being polite.

His tone held a definite note of sincerity. "I wouldn't have asked if I wasn't interested."

She leaned back on the couch and folded her hands in her lap. "I just finished a session as an intern with social services before I flew here."

Then again, maybe she didn't want to get into it all. Stefano was the picture of success. His winery was thriving. She'd been awed by all the awards he'd won. They were displayed in the wine-tasting room. His wine had worldwide recognition. He'd never understand failure. And she didn't want him to think less of her.

"Jules, are you going to make me drag it out of you a little at a time?"

"No. Never mind. It's not important." She attempted to get up, but Stefano reached out to her.

"It is important." His tone was filled with concern. "If it wasn't, you wouldn't be trying to tell your sister about it with the wedding so close. Since you can't talk to her, talk to me. Maybe I can help."

She glanced up at him and wanted to believe that he could actually understand. That he wouldn't think less of her. Jules's heart told her one thing, but her mind said the opposite. She decided to follow her heart.

Unable to look him in the eyes, she ducked her head. "I got fired from my position. Well, I don't know if you can get fired from an internship, but I was asked not to return."

There. It was out there. The embarrassing truth. She was a failure.

When Stefano didn't say anything, she glanced up. In his eyes, she didn't see any signs of judgment—just compassion.

"I'm sure there has to be more to the story than that. What aren't you telling me?"

"I…I couldn't do things the way they wanted. The kids…they needed someone in their corner. And I couldn't stand by and say nothing. When I spoke up one too many times, the supervisor determined I wasn't suited for the position."

"Sounds to me like you were just following your heart."

"But don't you see, I can't do that type of work. I can't follow their rules and regulations blindly when they just don't make sense in every case. I know the rules are there for a reason, but sometimes exceptions need to be made."

"Did you ever think that you're letting your injured ego override everything else? You could help so many kids. I agree with your sister. You need to keep going and get your degree. Maybe you can bring about change to the system."

Why did she ever think that opening up to him would be a good idea? He wasn't any different from her sister. Sure, it hurt getting fired. No matter how nicely the woman at the office stated it, a firing was a firing. She was certain there were other occupations that she could be just as good at or better.

But switching her focus made her feel as though she were copping out somehow. And she didn't want to turn her back on those kids who didn't have a voice. She wanted to do her part, but how could she do that without compromising who she was and what she believed in? She'd never be a yes-girl.

Guilt chewed at her as she considered doing something other than being a social worker. Why the guilt? Was it projected on her from her sister and now Stefano? She didn't know, but she sure wanted to figure it out. And she'd do it on her own, without his input or her sister's. This was a choice only she could make.

"Maybe you're right," she said. When he smiled broadly as though he'd just solved the world's economic crisis, she added, "But maybe you're not. That's why I haven't pressed the subject with Lizzie. I want to be sure before I get into it with her."

"And that's why what happened between us can't happen again."

Jules forced her mouth closed as a hundred thoughts struck her all at the same time. "You think me changing my mind about grad school is somehow related to us making love?"

"I think that you don't know what you want in life, and I don't want to confuse matters. It isn't like I can offer you anything serious. I've done that, and it didn't work out. You're still young. You have your whole future ahead of you."

A future without him. The thought tore through her, making the backs of her eyes sting. She blinked. He was right. They didn't have a future, but it had nothing to do with her being young or his first marriage ending. It had to do with her not being wife and mother material. Maybe he realized that, too, but didn't want to point it out.

Jules sucked in a steadying breath. "You're right. I have my whole future ahead of me. And right now that consists of creating the most amazing wedding for my sister."

She got to her feet and started for the door. No matter his reason for rejecting her and their lovemaking, it still hurt. She didn't want him to see how much it bothered her.

"This isn't how I meant for things to go between us." His voice was gentle and thick as honey. "Don't go away mad."

"Just go away," she mumbled.

She fled from the room as quickly as her legs would carry her. Her heart was heavy. He regretted their lovemaking, while she'd been replaying it over and over in her mind. She'd been such a fool to think that it'd been special for the both of them.

She wouldn't make that mistake again. And she didn't have time to dwell on her foolish mistake. The wedding was getting close—a wedding to top all others. It'd be so romantic that it'd have couples falling in love all over again.

Except for her and Stefano.

CHAPTER FOURTEEN

HE'D MADE A mess of everything.

Stefano's hands balled up and pounded the desktop, rattling the mug of pens as well as the computer keyboard. A few days had passed since he'd ended things with Jules. She still spoke to him, but it was at a bare minimum. And now that the wine-tasting event was over, he had far too much time on his hands.

What had gotten into him to let things get so out of control?

How could he have forgotten that his solitary life was one of his own making? His penance. If Jules had a clue he was to blame for his wife's death, she'd hate him. And that's how it should be. He didn't deserve another chance at love. And he certainly didn't deserve it at the expense of Jules's education. He couldn't stand to be responsible for the demise of her dreams. He'd done enough damage for one lifetime.

If only he'd kept his hands to himself. His

thoughts strayed back to the amazing time he'd spent with her wrapped in his arms. The strawberry scent of her hair. The velvety smoothness of her skin. He drew his tormenting thoughts up short. How could their lovemaking be so wrong when it felt so right?

It had to be all the talk about the wedding. It was messing with his mind, reminding him that he was all alone. Any other time that wouldn't have bothered him, but right now it sounded so grim and miserable. He was going to end up like his father. Old and alone.

But the memory of his father and Maria squeezed into his mind. Something told him that his father was starting to live again, step-by-step. He was happy for him, but that wasn't possible for Stefano. It was different.

Stefano had driven his wife from the house in the middle of the night with his unwillingness to compromise—his unwillingness to see that his wife was not the same woman he thought he'd married. Or that he'd only seen what he'd wanted to see when they'd said their vows. Either way, they'd both become disillusioned.

Her last words to him ran through his mind. *The man I thought I loved doesn't exist. He was a man I made up in my mind. We don't belong together. We never did.*

"Are you busy?"

The sound of Jules's voice had him turning to find her standing in the doorway of the winery office. "What are you doing here?"

Her eyes widened at his unintentionally brusque tone. "I wanted to know if you'd have time to run into the city tomorrow. But don't worry about it. I'll find another ride."

"Don't be silly. It's my responsibility to get you around." He hadn't meant to be so rough with her. He was frustrated with himself, not with her.

"I don't want to put you out. With you being busy, I can get there on the train."

In truth, he didn't have that much to do. This wasn't their busy time, and his father was moving around the vineyard like a man half his age. If it was because of Maria, he would be the first to admit that love suited his father. "I said I'd take you."

"Fine." She turned to walk away.

Guilt gnawed at him. He couldn't let her leave with things so tense between them. He couldn't stand the thought of her hating him. After all, they were going to be family.

He jumped to his feet and took off after her. "Hey, I'm sorry. I just have a lot on my mind right now."

She shrugged. "Don't worry about it. I know I've been a bother. Always getting in the way—"

"No, you haven't. You haven't done a thing

wrong." He didn't want this cold indifference to drag on. "I know I've been tough to live with lately. Let me make it up to you."

"You don't have to bother."

"But I want to."

"I don't know." She wrung her hands together. "What do you have in mind?"

He thought back to what she'd said about wanting a family and a menagerie of animals. He couldn't help her with the family, but there were animals at the vineyard. "How would you feel about a horseback ride around the grounds?"

She worried her bottom lip. "But I've never been on a horse before."

"I'll teach you."

Her eyes lit up. "Are you serious?"

He nodded. "Does this mean you agree?"

"I suppose."

Was that a hint of a smile pulling at her very tempting lips? He sure hoped so.

He suddenly found himself anxious to show her the ropes. Jules could be a lot of fun—when she wasn't upset with him. She had a way of making him smile, and it'd been a long time since he'd done that. The guy he used to be—the one who used to talk smoothly with the women and make them smile—now seemed like a stranger to him. Maybe it was time he brushed up on his skills. After all, there was no reason to make Jules miserable. She hadn't done anything wrong except get involved with him.

And how could things go astray while taking a horseback ride? After all, they'd be on separate horses. It wasn't like he would have a chance to wrap his arms around her and pull her close. Her lips wouldn't be right there in front of him, ripe for the picking.

He squelched the titillating thoughts. He had to see Jules like he saw other women. He couldn't keep lusting after her. Her future was in New York.

Jules was proud of herself.

After some coaching from Stefano and the patience of a mild-mannered horse, she was feeling at ease as Stefano guided her around the vineyard. The place was even bigger than she'd imagined. Acres and acres of vines stretched out in every direction. Stefano regaled her with stories of his family's history on the land and how they'd been able to expand onto neighboring lands.

She really enjoyed listening to him talk. She wasn't so sure if it was the honeyed tones of his voice or the entertaining twist he put on the tales—each story bigger and more outrageous than the last. He got her to laugh, and it felt good. It was as if a dark cloud had rolled away, letting the warm sunshine rain down on them.

They stopped on a distant hillside overlooking the villa. She wished that she'd brought her camera. This was a scene worthy of being on the back of a postcard. On the other side it should read: heaven.

Stefano alighted from Bandit, his chestnut mare with the fiery mane. The horse was spirited just like her master. And when they rode, it was if they could read each other's thoughts. Their ride had been smooth, and Jules had enjoyed watching them.

Stefano glanced her way as though waiting for her to get down. She wasn't about to budge, not a chance. Not without his help. She didn't relish the thought of falling on her backside, especially in front of him. She'd never live it down.

He started toward her. "Would you like some help?"

"Yes. Thank you."

When he stood before her, she leaned over. His hands gripped her waist as though they belonged there. Her fingers pressed to his muscled shoulders. The heat of his body permeated his shirt and warmed her hands. Her gaze met his. Her heart *tap-tapped*. She felt herself drowning in his bottomless eyes. The breath hitched in her throat as her body slid slowly, agonizingly, down over him.

When they stood chest to chest, there was a distinct unsteadiness in his breath. And then there was a nudge behind her. The horse had given her a healthy shove until her entire body was pressed against Stefano's unmoving form. In the next instance, his mouth pressed to hers. It was only then that she was willing to admit how much she'd longed for this moment.

His mouth moved passionately over hers as though he was starving for this kiss—for her. Her heart pounded in her chest. And the only thought in her head was the L word. Dare she admit it? How could she not?

She loved Stefano!

When had that happened? She wasn't sure. But she knew it'd been growing and evolving for a while now. And she couldn't deny it any longer. She was in love with Stefano DeFiore. Her heart soared as she met his kiss with her own vigor and excitement.

She felt as though she were floating on a fluffy cloud. She didn't want to mess up this moment. She'd been waiting her whole life for him. Wrapped in his arms, it felt as though anything was possible. And it didn't matter how steep the climb—she would reach the summit. She could do it.

Before she lost her nerve, she had to tell him. She had to let him know that she loved him with all her heart. Her insides quivered, and she didn't know if it was the excitement of his kiss or the trepidation of vocalizing the L word—something she hadn't said since she was a naive kid.

Using every bit of willpower, she braced her hands on his solid chest and pushed. Her mouth tingled, but she resisted the urge to smooth her fingers over the whisker-worn skin. There was a far more important task ahead of her. She hoped he felt the same way about her.

His confused gaze met hers. She couldn't let him say anything. He'd ruin the moment, and she'd lose her nerve.

"I love you."

Those three ginormous words hung there. Stefano didn't move. He didn't speak. She wasn't even sure if he was still breathing.

As the silence stretched on, she started to question whether she'd truly uttered the words or just imagined the whole thing.

"Did you hear me?" She didn't have the courage to repeat the words.

His eyes darkened. He'd heard her. And he wasn't going to respond the way she'd imagined—the way she'd hoped he would.

His hands fell away from her, setting her free. In fact, it was as though he'd quickly erected a fortress around himself. He didn't even have to say anything; she already felt the coldness of rejection.

She refused to let him off that easily. She'd

never spoken those words to another man in her entire life. He at least owed her an explanation of his feelings. A simple apology because he didn't feel the same way. Anything but this damnable silence that was about to drive her crazy.

"Say something!" She clenched her fists. "Don't just ignore me."

He cleared his throat. "I'm not."

"Aren't you going to say anything in response?"

His hands moved to his waist and he stared down at the ground. "I can't tell you what you think you want to hear."

Wait. Did he just say what she thought he'd said? She replayed his words in her mind.

"What I *think* I want you to say. What does that mean?"

He sighed. "You're a long way from home. Your sister is moving half a globe away from you. And you're at a crossroads in your life. It's natural that you'd want to reach out to someone and hold on tight. It would be an easy fix."

With every word out of his mouth her face warmed, but it wasn't embarrassment. It was anger. He was diminishing this moment—the first time she'd trusted a man with her heart. And he was shredding it before handing it back to her.

Unable to formulate words, she stood there. Tears stung her eyes, and she blinked repeatedly, refusing to let them fall. She was stronger than that. Stefano didn't deserve to witness her tears.

"You don't love me." He shifted his weight from one foot to the other. "I'm flattered that you think so highly of me, but if you really knew me, you wouldn't love me."

He wasn't getting off that easily. "Tell me. Tell me every reason that would make you unlovable."

He shook his head and then rubbed the back of his neck. "I don't think so. We need to get back to the villa before people start to wonder what happened to us."

"I'm not going anywhere until you talk to me." She walked over to a tall tree filled with fluttering green leaves and sank down on the lush grass beneath it.

"Jules, be reasonable."

"I am. I was honest about my feelings. Now you need to be honest with me. I'm not going anywhere until you do."

Resignation filtered across his tanned face. He led the horses over to a nearby tree and tied them up before returning to her side. He sat down next to her.

She steeled herself for whatever he was about to say. The way he'd been acting and holding himself back told her that it was pretty serious. Whatever it was, they'd deal with it together.

"Talk to me, Stefano. I've told you about my past."

"I know you did, and I appreciate how brave you were to do that, but this isn't the same thing. I…" He plucked a piece of tall grass and twirled it between his fingers. "I've done things—things that can't be forgiven."

She wanted to understand, but he wasn't giving her much to go on. "Does this have to do with your wife?"

He nodded. "We were high school sweethearts. She had this special way about her. All the guys turned to watch when she passed by, but she only had eyes for me."

"What was she like?"

"A dreamer. She'd love to lie back in the grass and stare up at the blue sky and talk about her dreams for the future." He leaned back against the trunk of the tree. "Taking those dreams from her changed her."

"How did you do that?"

"I married her. She thought by marrying a De-Fiore that my money would bankroll her dreams. The truth is she never wanted to live here at the vineyard. She longed for the city and the high life."

"And you didn't see things that way?"

"No." Stefano gazed straight ahead. "After the honeymoon ended, the arguments started. She wanted to travel, and I kept putting her off, hoping she'd adjust to our new life together."

"But she never did."

He shook his head. "And I thought if we had a baby that it'd help things." He raked his fingers through his hair. "I don't know what I was thinking. A baby is no answer to problems in a marriage, but I was desperate. We were becoming more distant by the day."

Jules knew that it was important for him to get this off his chest and for her to hear it. She also knew how difficult and painful it could be to peel back the scab on a deep wound. She reached out and squeezed his hand, giving him what reassurance she could.

He cleared his throat. "Nothing I said or did was right. And I was losing hope that somehow we'd find the light at the end of the tunnel."

"Oh, Stefano. I'm so sorry. It must have been so hard for you."

"But that's just it—it shouldn't have been so hard. If only we'd talked before we got married. I mean really talked about what we were feeling and what we wanted out of life. But we were always so busy with this or that. I kept putting it off, figuring that we were in love and that life would just work itself out. But I was so wrong. I really messed things up."

"I'm sure you aren't the only one who thought

that love was enough to iron out all of the wrinkles in life. Sometimes love runs out of steam and the wrinkles are all that remain."

He turned to her, his eyes full of turmoil. "But it's more than that. When I learned that Gianna wasn't interested in having kids or living here at the vineyard, I didn't take it well. I thought when we married that it was understood that we would start a family and I would keep working at the winery."

"But she wanted her dreams, and they were a long way from the vineyard."

He nodded. "She wanted to travel the world and write stories of our experiences. She said there were people that became professional bloggers for a living. She thought since I did well in English class that I would be able to do this. What she didn't consider was that I hate to write. I can do it for the winery blog, but it is out of necessity, not want."

To Jules, he was a hands-on guy, one who didn't mind rolling up his sleeves and getting dirty—actually he probably preferred it. As for kids, Jules imagined he'd make an excellent father. He had the patience and the temperament to help them reach their full potential. If only she could be like that… But this wasn't about her, and there was more to his story. Of that she was certain.

"What happened to your wife?"

"Things had been deteriorating between us for a long time. I'd finally moved into the bedroom next to hers. She'd threatened to leave numerous times, and I always talked her out of it, certain that there had to be a way to fix things. But I just didn't know what the answer was." He sighed deeply as though he'd been carrying around the weight of the world on his shoulders. "Then one stormy night, she prepared dinner, but I could tell that she had something on her mind. Neither of us ate much, and when my father made a quick exit to his room, her anger and frustration came tumbling out. She said that she got an email from one of our classmates, and he was about to set sail around the world."

Jules's insides tensed with foreboding. His tone grew softer as though he had disappeared back in time to that fateful night. She wanted to pull him back to her—back to the present—but she couldn't. If they were ever going to make a future for themselves, then they had to get this all out in the open.

"What…what happened next?"

He gave Jules a quick glance as though she'd startled him back to reality. Then, in a hollow, pained voice, he continued, "Gianna said that she was tired of waiting for me. She was losing time, time that she could be off exploring the world, discovering new things. I...I asked her if she still loved me."

Jules's heart pinched. She knew the answer, and she was willing to bet that he'd known the answer before he had even asked the question. The backs of her eyes stung again, and she blinked repeatedly to keep her tears of sympathy from splashing down her cheeks. She didn't want to make this any harder on him.

He drew in an unsteady breath. "She said she didn't love me. She...she didn't know if she ever truly did because I wasn't the man she thought she'd married."

Jules squeezed his hand tight. She wanted to offer words of comfort, of encouragement, but they clogged up in her throat. This story was going to get worse, much worse. She lifted her head and tried to subdue her emotions. In the otherwise clear blue sky, one lone cloud floated over them, blocking out the sunlight.

Stefano massaged the back of his neck. "I was hurt and I was angry. Most of all, I was tired— tired of all the fighting. Tired of trying to find a way out of the mess. Tired of feeling so miserable. And that's when I made the worst mistake of my life."

The air was trapped in Jules's lungs as she waited for what happened next—what had turned this fine man into a shadow of the outgoing person everyone told her he used to be.

"I told Gianna that I wasn't a man to skip off into the sunset and forget my responsibilities. And that she might as well quit waiting around for that to happen. If she didn't love me or our life at the vineyard, then she could use the door. I told her I was done...with her." He rubbed a hand over his eyes. "And with our marriage." He dropped his face into his hands. "Why did I do that?"

"You can't blame yourself for being honest with her."

His head jerked up, and his distraught gaze needled her. "You don't know what you're saying. If only I hadn't lost my patience—if I'd tried to reason with her, none of it would have happened."

"What happened?"

The only sound was the breeze rustling the leaves overhead and a couple of birds singing. Stefano stared off into the distant horizon as though in his mind he was back in that stormy night. Jules waited for the ominous conclusion to his heart-wrenching story.

"For the first time ever, she didn't fight back." His voice cracked with emotion. "It was as though my words had knocked the fight out of her. Gianna ran out of the kitchen. I didn't want to go upstairs. I didn't want to confront her again. So I started cleaning up the dinner dishes. I don't know how much time passed when I heard the car start and the engine rev as she gassed it out of the driveway. I went to the door and ran outside after her. The rain was coming down in sheets, and the wind was turbulent. It wasn't a night fit for driving. But I couldn't stop her."

Jules's wrapped her arm around his back and leaned her head against his shoulder. "You didn't force her out into the storm—"

"But I did. I was the reason she ran off that night. I didn't give her any reason to stay. If only I'd…"

"Nothing you could have said would have made a difference. She was only waiting for you to give her a reason to follow through with her threats. She wanted to go."

"But not that night." His voice cracked with emotion. "It wasn't too much later when the phone rang. The car had hydroplaned…Gianna lost control. The…the car went over an embankment."

How awful. Now Jules understood the shadow that seemed to follow him around and the way he pulled back when he was having a good time.

"It's not your fault," she repeated, willing him to believe her. "She knew what she was doing."

"But she wouldn't have been out there if I had thought before opening my mouth. I had all of those months to tell her how I was feeling. Why did it have to be that night?"

"Because she was backing you into a corner. She wanted to go, but she just hadn't worked up the courage to do it."

"So you agree. I'm responsible—"

"No. That's not what I'm saying. You'll never know exactly what she was thinking that night. But she was a grown woman plenty capable of making her own choices and the accident was just that—an accident."

"They said that she died instantly." His voice was so soft that she strained to hear him. "The coroner said she was pregnant. She was going to have my baby." A tear splashed onto his cheek.

Jules leaned forward and wrapped her arms around him. At first, he hesitated, and then his body pressed against hers. Her heart was breaking for him. When he finally got himself together, he pulled back. She reluctantly let him go.

She looked into his bloodshot eyes. "And this is the guilt you've been carrying around with you, isn't it? Every time we start to get close, you pull back because you're still blaming yourself for Gianna and the baby?"

"Yes." His voice took on a weary, broken tone. "I don't deserve to have you in my life."

"I disagree. I think I'm exactly what you need."

When he glanced at her, she ducked her head and pressed her lips to his. He didn't move at first. She brushed her mouth over his, hoping he'd respond—that he'd reach out to her. He'd been so alone for so long and piling on the guilt for his wife's untimely death. She couldn't imagine what that would feel like. He was a good guy, and he deserved to move on with his life.

His lips moved over hers like a drowning man sucking in some much needed oxygen. He pulled her over onto his lap. His hands on either side of her head. Her hands resting on his powerful shoulders. Lip to lip and tongue to tongue, the love dance of a lifetime started.

At last the wall between them had come crumbling down. Jules knew what she wanted—Stefano. She wanted all of him, his past and his future. She loved him.

CHAPTER FIFTEEN

"We shouldn't have done that." Stefano rushed to button his shirt.

He swore under his breath. Every time he was alone with Jules all his common sense evaporated. Guilt consumed him. He'd meant to explain to her why they couldn't be together and he'd ended up making love to her instead.

He raked his fingers through his hair. He didn't dare look at her. It would be so easy to believe this was the beginning of something—not the end of something very special. *Wait.* Why was she taking this so well? She should be yelling at him—calling him every rotten name in the book. After all, he'd be the first to admit that he deserved it.

Maybe she hadn't heard him. That had to be it. He opened his mouth to repeat himself, but nothing came out. He pressed his lips together. Deep down he didn't want to push Jules away—he wanted to pull her close and keep her there.

But that was impossible. And now, after reliving how his lack of good judgment had cost Gianna and their unborn child their lives, he couldn't do the same thing with Jules's future. He couldn't let her wreck her future over him.

No matter how much she'd end up hating him, he had to set Jules free. It was for the best. "I'm sorry—"

"Don't be. You were amazing." Jules pulled on her boots and strode over to him. She smiled up at him. "And I—"

He pressed a finger to her soft lips, not letting her finish. He knew what she was going to say, and he didn't think that he could bear to hear her say again that she loved him. If she uttered those words, he was afraid the last of his resolve would crack, and that couldn't happen.

"You aren't understanding me." He averted his face to avoid witnessing the inevitable hurt in her eyes. "You and I aren't meant to be."

"Yes, we are."

"No, we aren't. Your life is back in New York. You have grad school to attend."

"Grad school was Lizzie's idea, not mine. I want to stay here with you."

He couldn't keep arguing with her. She had to understand that this thing, whatever it was, wasn't going to happen again. She had a life to lead, and it wasn't with him.

Stefano grasped her shoulders. "You have to hear me. This thing between us is over. After the wedding, you'll get on a plane back to New York and I'll be busy preparing for the harvest."

Her eyes opened wide. "You're serious, aren't you?"

"Yes, I am."

"But we just shared—"

"A special moment that I'll never forget. But we have to be realistic. We both want different things in the future. And you don't even know for certain what that's going to be."

She drew her shoulders back. Her eyes glittered with strength and determination. "I know I want you. And you punishing yourself for your wife's accident isn't going to change what happened. You're a good man, and you deserve to be happy again."

"I will be when I know that you aren't throwing away your future. You have the whole world at your feet. All you have to do is choose your path."

"I choose you."

He refused to accept her words. She didn't mean them. In time, she would realize that they were a mistake. "Don't let your experience as an intern scare you away from grad school. This world needs people who see things that need changing and aren't afraid to speak up. The key is not to give up in the face of adversity. Sometimes you just have to regroup and take a different approach. Be the voice of those children who can't speak for themselves."

She hadn't thought of it that way. Was she turning her back on helping countless children who didn't have a voice? The thought tumbled through her mind.

"And if you want to be a mother, you can do that, too. Don't let your past hold you back. I know your life with your mother wasn't good, but use it as a lesson in what not to do as a parent."

Jules worried her lush bottom lip. "But what if I'm no good at it?"

"Follow your heart. It won't lead you astray. You have good instincts. If you do that, you can't possibly fail. But remember that no one is perfect. You'll make mistakes along the way. Everyone does. Just learn from them."

She tilted her head to the side and gave him a hard stare. "You know, you're awfully full of good advice for a bachelor."

"You forget I come from a very big family, and they are all full of advice. I guess some of it rubbed off on me."

She was going to make someone an amazing wife. And when the time came some child was going to be showered in love. The image of her with a husband and baby flashed in his mind, causing his gut to knot up.

"To bad you can't accept advice as well as you hand it out." Her lips pressed into a hard line.

His hand rubbed over his stubbled jaw as a war raged inside him. "I wish I could tell you what you want to hear. But I can't."

"And here's my advice to you. Don't let the past dictate your future. Live in the moment. Otherwise you're going to miss everything that is good in life." When he didn't say anything, she glared at him. "Why do I even try? I give up."

The pained look in her eyes stabbed deep into his heart. He'd rather have dealt with some female hysterics than the defeat that was reflected in her expression. She turned, glanced over at the horses and then started walking back to the villa.

"Don't you want to ride?" he called out to her retreating form.

She shook her head and picked up her pace.

He started after her. He couldn't let it end this way. He had to tell her that their lovemaking had meant so much more than he was letting on. It had moved his world and left him wanting more of her.

His steps slowed down. He couldn't do that. He'd be encouraging her to stay here with him. She'd sacrifice everything. And maybe not today or tomorrow but someday she'd regret it. And she'd blame him.

He stopped. His gaze followed her. He assured himself that this was best for both of them. No matter how much the sacrifice would cost him.

Because beneath it all, he loved her.

In the days that ensued, Jules resolved to hold Stefano at arm's length.

How could she have been so foolish to think that he felt the same way about her? How many times had she been told that men and women looked at relationships two different ways? She knew better. While she was busy letting her heart fill with love for him, he was enjoying the moment. He wasn't picturing a future with a picket fence, two-point-five kids and a cat or two or three.

She nuzzled Apricot close to her neck. "You know I'm leaving soon. The wedding is next week. And then my time here will be over."

Apricot purred and used her tiny pin-like nails to climb up on Jules's shoulder, where she liked to perch. The kitten's happy meter went all the way to the top, and all Jules could hear was the sound of purring. Jules loved the sound. It was comforting and reassuring. Boy, was she going to miss Apricot, this vineyard and—

She brought her thoughts up short. She refused

to miss Stefano. He was the one to turn away from her—to dismiss their lovemaking as if it meant nothing. And to think that she'd blurted out that she loved him. She blinked rapidly. No way was she going to cry. He didn't deserve her tears.

Wedding or no wedding, she didn't know if she'd be able to face him again. There were just some things that you couldn't take back once they were spoken. A frustrated growl rose in her throat. Why, oh, why had she thought Stefano had been the exception to her rule about not trusting people with her heart?

Her fingers ran over Apricot's downy-soft fur. There was something so comforting and reassuring about a fur baby's presence. It calmed her and let her realize that she was wasting her time standing around thinking about Stefano. He was going to be Lizzie's in-law, and that was all. She'd probably never see him again. Well, that might be stretching it a bit, but their run-ins would be few and far between.

Speaking of which, she was supposed to ride with him to Rome for the final dress fitting. Her stomach knotted up thinking of sitting next to him—alone with him—for the entire ride. That wasn't going to happen. She'd get to Rome some other way.

A glance at the time told her that she had to get a move on. A red-and-white-striped sundress flirted just above her knees. The new white-heeled sandals perfectly complemented the dress. She had to admit that it was a big stretch from her usual black-and-purple ensembles, but she was finding that she was having fun with colors. Maybe she'd hemmed her fashion choices in too tightly. She was actually quite comfortable in the dress. Of course, she'd applied makeup to cover up her scars, but she hadn't gone so heavy with the eye makeup. Maybe when she went back to New York, she would maintain this makeover. Or at least switch up her wardrobe now and then.

She reached up and removed Apricot from her shoulder. "You have to be good, okay?"

Those big blue eyes stared at her, looking as innocent as could be. But Jules knew what trouble this fur baby could get herself into from climbing up on furniture and being unsure how to get down to sticking her paw in a glass of water and tipping it over.

"We'll just see if Massimo is up to keeping an eye on you. He'll make sure you don't get into too much trouble while I'm gone. And you can entertain him. I don't know why, but he certainly seems to like you, little miss."

Apricot mewed as if she knew what Jules had said to her.

With a smile, Jules headed downstairs in search of Massimo. Since his stroke, his room was on the first floor, and he spent a lot of time in the living room with the large glass wall that made the room bright and cheery. And that's exactly where she found him. He was sitting on the couch doing a crossword puzzle. He glanced up and sent her a lopsided smile.

"I see you brought the fuzzy one to visit."

"Yes, Apricot is feeling particularly energetic. I was wondering if you could keep an eye on her while I go to Rome. Today is our last dress fitting."

"Ah, my grandson will be driving you."

"I think I'll take the train. He has work to do."

"DeFiore men don't put work ahead of their obligations to beautiful women." Massimo reached out and squeezed her hand. "I know something is troubling you. Just remember that anything worth having is worth fighting for. Life isn't easy, and the good stuff doesn't just land in your lap. You have to work for it and never give up."

"Are you ready to go?"

She turned to find Stefano standing in the hallway. His face was a mask of indifference. It was the first time they'd spoken to each other since their moment on the grassy hillside.

"If you'd just drop me at the train station, I'll be fine."

"Don't be ridiculous. I said that I would take

you, and I'm ready to go. Besides, there isn't another train until much later."

She sighed. The last thing she wanted to do was end up in a fight with him. "I was just asking your grandfather if he'd keep an eye on Apricot."

"I'd love to." Massimo reached out for the fluff ball, and she gently placed the squirming kitten in his hands.

"I should run and get her food bowl."

"No need. I'm sure Maria won't mind getting some food."

Jules glanced around, spotting the litter box in the corner of the room. "And water. I forgot the water."

"Don't worry. We'll be fine together."

"Are you sure?"

Massimo sent her a reassuring smile. "Go before you're late for your appointment. Did you say this was the last fitting?"

She nodded. "We're taking our dresses home today. Well, I guess I'm bringing both dresses here as Lizzie doesn't want to take any chance on Dante spotting it."

"All the more reason for me to drive you," Stefano piped in. "The dresses would get wrinkled on the train or worse."

He did have a good point. "Then we best get going."

This was going to be the longest ride of her life.

There was tangible tension between them, and she didn't know how to get around it. She didn't even know if she wanted to resolve it. After all, she hadn't started any of this. It was Stefano. One minute he wanted her, and the next he was shoving her away and spouting out every reason why they shouldn't be together.

If he thought she was the only one who didn't know what she wanted, then he should take a good look in the mirror. His mouth said one thing. But his body said another.

CHAPTER SIXTEEN

WHAT WAS TAKING SO LONG?

Stefano sat alone in the front of the bridal boutique. The oval table in front of him was littered with every bridal magazine published. No matter how bored he was, there was no way he was picking up one of those periodicals. He'd had his fill of flowers, dresses and cakes.

He glanced at his wristwatch for the second time in five minutes. Jules and Lizzie were supposed to try on their dresses and then they'd be on their way. Not that he was anxious to repeat the car ride with Jules. The whole ride to Rome had been nothing but tense silence. What should he say to her? That he was sorry? That when he was around her he couldn't think straight? That he cared so much about her that he was trying to protect her from himself?

It was all true. But he couldn't take back his words. She'd never believe him. And if she did, where would that leave them?

His temples started to throb. Oh, it didn't matter what he felt for her. Just speaking the words that she meant something to him would only spur her on to stay here, and then what? One day she'd wake and realize that she'd sacrificed everything for him, and then she'd leave. She'd go off to follow her dreams.

It was best to let her go now before they got in too deep. He knew that she cared for him, but it wasn't as if they'd made promises to each other. The exit door was still wide-open for both of them. By giving her a healthy shove through it, he was doing her a big favor. She may not realize it now, but in time she would understand.

She'd return to her life in New York—to grad school—and she'd soon forget about him. His gut churned. With her beauty, she could have her choice of men.

At last, the women stepped into the waiting area. Each was carrying a white zippered garment bag. They were chatting back and forth. Neither even seemed to notice him. He didn't know why it should bother him. He was, after all, just the chauffeur. And this was what he wanted—Jules to forget about him—wasn't it?

He shifted uncomfortably in his seat, not sure if they were leaving or if there was more that needed to be done. When Lizzie's phone buzzed, she held up a finger to Jules to wait a moment.

Jules glanced over at him. When she didn't move, he did. He strode over and held out his hand. "Let me take that for you."

She didn't say a word as she handed over the dress. Once she'd adjusted it so that it wouldn't wrinkle, she turned and picked up a bridal magazine. As though he wasn't even in the room, she thumbed through the glossy pages.

He'd been privy to all the other stuff for the wedding except the dresses. He had to admit he was really curious to see what Jules would be wearing. Would it be purple like the paper flowers he'd helped her make? Or would it be another color? Was it short, showing off her legs? Or was it longer on the bottom with the top scaled back and showing off her bare shoulders and that butterfly on her chest?

He cut off his thoughts. They were only going to get him in trouble. What Jules wore to the wedding made no difference to him. He inwardly groaned, wishing that were the case.

"Are you ready to go?" He hoped so. The tension was starting to give him a headache.

She glanced up. "Are you that anxious to get away from me?"

"Of course not."

She turned back to the magazine. "I could take the train back. You don't have to wait if you're that anxious to go."

"Would you stop putting words in my mouth? I just wanted to know if I should take the dress to the car."

"Oh." She glanced down at the earth-tone swirls of the plush carpeting.

How in the world had they gone from laughter and kissing among other delicious things to this awkward silence? Agitation churned in his gut. He knew the answer, and he didn't like it one bit. He'd let things get out of hand. When he'd tried to fix it, it was too late. And he'd only made things worse.

Lizzie approached them. "That was Dante. He needs me right away at the restaurant. Something's come up. Do you think you could handle picking out the candles for the tables? I'm really sorry about this."

More time together. More stress and tension. Stefano's body grew rigid.

"Sure." Jules wore a smile that didn't reach her eyes. "Do you need anything else?"

"Not that I can think of." Lizzie gave her a hug. "You've been great. I don't know what I'd have done without you. I'm really going to miss you when you leave for school."

"I'm sure you'll be so busy being a newlywed that you won't even notice."

Lizzie beamed. "I think you're right. Oh, there is one more thing. Would you mind stopping by the florist? They called and said that one of the flowers they ordered is out of stock or some such thing. Anyway, they said they had a suitable replacement, but I haven't had a chance to stop by. Would you mind?"

This was the last straw. Stefano just couldn't take it anymore. Everyone was acting as if everything was perfect, and it wasn't. Nothing about this was right. Jules was hiding the truth from her sister, and her sister was taking advantage of Jules's guilt and generosity.

"Yes, she minds," he heard himself say. "She's been running herself ragged for you because of that television show, and she can't do everything. You need to stop taking advantage of Jules and listen to what she needs and wants."

Both women gaped at him as if he'd just sprouted another head. But he didn't care at this point. Lizzie didn't know how much it was costing Jules to spend time in the car with him. He could tell that she just wanted to get away from him.

Jules stepped up to him and poked a finger at his chest. "You're the pot calling the kettle black. Who are you to tell Lizzie that when you refuse to hear what I've been telling you? You are so caught up in trying to make up for the past that you can't see what's right in front of you. You're squandering your future, and it's for nothing. You did nothing wrong." Her shoulders hunched as she shook her head. "I don't know why I'm wasting my time. You refuse to accept anything I say."

He wanted to object, but he couldn't. Was she right? Was it time to let go of the past? Could he move past the guilt?

Jules snatched the dress from him and turned her back to him. "Come on, Lizzie."

At the sight of her retreating back, he once again found his voice. "Jules, wait."

She stopped and turned, giving him an icy, pointed stare that stabbed straight through to his heart. "Lizzie, I need someplace to stay tonight."

"Umm…sure. Whatever you need." Lizzie frowned at him. When he went to approach Jules, who was already pulling the front door open, Lizzie held up her palm, stopping him in his tracks. "Let her go."

He blew out a pent-up breath as he raked his fingers through his hair. He'd blown it. He'd meant to help Jules and instead he'd opened his mouth and inserted his size-twelve shoe. Once upon a time he'd been good at talking to the ladies, but lately he just never seemed to say the right thing. At least not where Jules was concerned.

Still he couldn't stand the thought of her hating him. He had to say something. Whether or not it would help things he didn't know. "I'm sorry."

The glass door swung shut, and his words were lost in the warm breeze. Oh, man, what had he done? He rubbed the back of his neck, trying to gather himself. How had things ended up in such a jumbled mess? The truth was he'd ended up causing Jules the very same pain he'd been trying to save her from.

He had to stop them. He had to try again to apologize. But he was too late. He stopped on the sidewalk and didn't see the women anywhere. It was as though they'd vanished.

When Dante heard about this he'd be lucky if he didn't drive to the vineyard and kick him around the villa. And, frankly, he couldn't blame his brother. He'd utterly screwed up everything.

Late the following morning, Jules strolled to the living room of Dante and Lizzie's very spacious apartment. She hoped that she'd slept late enough that her sister would be downstairs at Ristorante Massimo.

"About time you woke up." Lizzie's voice echoed across the room. "I was starting to get worried about you." She held up a mug. "Would you like some caffeine?"

Jules yawned as she nodded her head. She'd been up most of the night thinking about Stefano and wondering what his outburst at the bridal boutique had been about. What in the world had gotten into him to say those things?

And what was Lizzie thinking? Yesterday her sister had been unusually quiet and hadn't brought up Stefano at all. Of course, some of that might have had to do with Jules fighting back tears. Maybe she didn't want to make matters worse.

But today was a new day, and Jules could feel her sister's inquisitive gaze on her. Jules wished she'd just speak up and get it over with. She wasn't good with hedging around subjects. It just ended up unnerving her more.

"Say it." Jules plunked down on the couch.

"Say what?" Lizzie said innocently as she approached her with a steaming mug of coffee.

"Don't go acting like nothing happened. You want to know what was up with Stefano and me yesterday, don't you?"

"Since you brought it up, yes. I'd like to know how far this thing between you two has gone. Are you in love with him?"

Wow! Way to go straight to the heart of the matter. Pride refused to let Jules admit that she was in love with a man who didn't love her back. She'd already made a fool of herself in front of him; she couldn't do the same with her sister.

"No. I'm not." Guilt rained down on her.

Lizzie stared at her as though trying to make

up her mind. "And you still plan to attend grad school, right?"

What else did she have waiting for her back in New York? She might as well stick to her original plan. "Of course."

"Good. Because I just sent in the tuition payment."

Jules had totally forgotten about that. Well, it appeared that everyone was getting what they wanted. She would soon be out of Stefano's life, and she'd be going back to school just like her sister wanted. She should be happy that she was being offered such an amazing opportunity. Not everyone was so blessed. But somehow she just couldn't work up the excitement.

Now wasn't the time to dwell on things, not with the wedding in a matter of days. "Now that we have that settled—"

The phone rang, and Lizzie held up a finger, stopping Jules in midsentence. Jules was glad to have a small reprieve. She could use a healthy dose of caffeine before she dealt any more with her sister.

Jules swallowed another mouthful of the fragrant brew with a touch of cream and sweetener. She did have to admit that Italian coffee was quite good. In fact, she could easily get used to drinking it.

Over the rim of her cup, she noticed Lizzie

had moved to the galley kitchen. Her back was to her, and Jules could only make out a word here and there—not that she was trying to eavesdrop. She had enough of her own problems without dabbling into someone else's. As it was, she was quite certain that the Stefano issue hadn't been laid to rest that easily. Lizzie was never satisfied that quickly when she was concerned about something.

A few minutes later, Jules set her empty mug on the glass coffee table. Lizzie returned, taking a seat on the couch opposite hers. "That was Stefano on the phone."

Jules was tempted to ask what he wanted, but she resisted the urge. Her sister's inquisitive stare bore into her. She had no doubt that Lizzie knew how much it was killing her not to ask about him, but she had to play this right or Lizzie would turn into a protective mother bear. She'd make matters worse for everyone. And with the wedding just around the corner, drama was the last thing any of them needed.

Lizzie curled her feet up on the black leather couch and sipped her coffee. Waiting for her sister to speak was pure torture. At her breaking point, Jules asked, "What did he want?"

"He called to apologize."

"That's good. He should. He knows nothing about you and me."

Lizzie's lips pressed together in a firm line and her brows gathered. "He wanted to talk to you, but I told him that you didn't want to talk to him yet. That is right, isn't it?"

He wanted to talk to her? She wondered what he wanted to say. Then she realized with the pending wedding that he probably just wanted to apologize and smooth things over before the big day. The thought dashed her hopes that he might have miraculously come to his senses.

"That's fine. I can talk to him when I get back to the vineyard, anyway. I have a lot to do when I get there. The temporary flooring and tent will be arriving tomorrow, and I have to figure out the most level spot to set everything up. I should grab my planner and we can go over the final details."

She went to stand when Lizzie said, "Wait. We aren't done talking."

Jules sighed as she settled back on the couch.

"What did Stefano mean by I don't listen to you?"

No way was she getting into all of this with Lizzie on the week of her wedding. This was Lizzie's moment to shine. There would be a better time and place for this talk.

Jules shrugged. "I don't know. I think he was just frustrated. This running around for the wedding while trying to keep his business going has been a lot for him. I think he just needed to blow off some steam."

"That's interesting because he said almost the same thing on the phone."

"He did? I mean—see? I was right. Don't worry. Everything will be fine. All you have to do is show up for the big day." She forced a smile.

"You better not be falling for him." Lizzie gave her an I-mean-business look. "You can't mess up grad school. You worked too hard for it."

And you already paid the tuition.

Jules stifled a frustrated sigh. Time to change the subject.

"By the way, where's Dante?"

CHAPTER SEVENTEEN

"ARE YOU TRYING to ruin everything?"

Stefano's body tensed at the sound of Dante's voice. His brother was the last person he wanted to deal with right now. He glanced up as Dante crossed the patio in his direction. Stefano turned away and stared blindly out over the sun-drenched rows of grapevines. The only vision in his mind was Jules's beautiful face.

"I'm not up for it today, Dante," Stefano warned.

"Too bad." The footsteps behind him stopped. "You have some explaining to do, big brother."

So he'd heard about the incident yesterday at the bridal boutique. He wasn't surprised, but the fact Dante had driven to the vineyard while the *ristorante* was open for business was a worrisome development.

Stefano sighed and turned to face his brother. "Shouldn't you be in Rome working?"

"I would be if my brother wasn't trying to wreck my wedding."

"What? I'm not doing any such thing."

"That's not what I hear." Dante's hands rested on his waist, pushing his suit jacket back. "I know that you're not a fan of weddings after what happened to you and Papa, but I thought you were man enough to step aside and let me make my own choices."

"I am. I did." How did he explain away yesterday? Jules wasn't even speaking to him. "How's Jules?"

"First, I think you owe me an explanation before I withdraw my request for you to be my best man."

The serious glint in Dante's eyes left Stefano no doubt about his sincerity. But he needed to know Jules was okay after the way she'd disappeared. "This is important. How's Jules? Did she say anything to you?"

Dante's brows arched. "You've fallen for her, haven't you?"

"No, I haven't. We're…we're friends. That's all."

"You have it real bad for her, and you're fighting it. That's what yesterday was about. And judging by Jules's tears, she has it bad for you, too."

"She was crying?"

His brother nodded.

Stefano ran a hand over his stubbled jaw. He

hadn't bothered to shave. This was worse than he'd been imagining. He wanted to go to her and take her in his arms. But he couldn't do that. It'd only succeed in making things worse. She'd get over him. She surely didn't love him, did she? It was a crush. Nothing more.

"You need to make this right." Dante's tone left no doubt about his sincerity. "And I don't mean by playing the part of Romeo. That's already gotten us in enough trouble."

He waved away his brother's unwanted advice. "I know. I know. You don't have to lecture me, little brother."

"Really? Because from where I'm standing you've made a mess of things. And this is my wedding week. My bride is not happy, and this should be the best time of her life."

"Okay. I hear you. I'll fix this."

"I'm glad to hear you say that." The stress lines on his brother's face eased. "Then quit messing around with my soon-to-be sister-in-law. You know she's supposed to go off to some grad school, don't you?"

"Yes, I know. I've been telling her that's what she should be concentrating on."

"I bet you have." Dante sent him an I-know-better-than-that look. "And Lizzie just paid the tuition. She's counting on Jules following through with this. Don't ruin this for Jules, or you'll have me to answer to."

Stefano had no doubt that Dante meant business. His brother wasn't about to let anything ruin his wedding, and Stefano couldn't blame him. He'd be the same way if he was marrying Jules—not that he would ever be walking down the aisle again.

The first thing he had to do was talk to Jules, but since she wasn't answering her phone and Lizzie was running interference, he'd have to wait until she returned to the villa.

He didn't know what he'd say to her aside from apologizing for making a fool of himself. Maybe that would be enough. He hoped.

Jules's insides quivered. She'd rather be doing anything but this. Even a trip to the dentist sounded good to her at this point.

Her footsteps were slow but steady as she entered the winery. Lizzie had loaned her a car to transport the dresses to the villa without incident. No one wanted to trust the dresses on the train. And now that the wedding gear was stowed away safely in a spare room, Jules had to face Stefano. Things couldn't linger like this. She'd promised Lizzie there would be peace for the wedding.

She'd made a fool of herself over Stefano, but she would be fine without him. She sucked in an unsteady breath. Her heart disagreed, but her mind kept telling her to do what was easiest for everyone.

When she found Stefano, he was in the barrel room, testing some wine. He glanced up and surprise registered in his dark eyes. Then it was as if a wall came down, making it impossible to know what he was thinking. She was shut out once again.

She refused to let it stop her. "Can we talk?"

He nodded. "I needed to talk to you, too."

"I promised my sister that you and I would make peace."

"I promised my brother the same thing."

That was a good sign, right? It was so hard to tell. He didn't smile. Did she always have such a hard time reading him?

She twisted her hands together. "I just wanted to let you know that I'll stay out of your way from now on. And I'll be leaving right after the wedding."

She turned to go, and he reached out for her arm. His touch was warm and gentle. It sent a current of electricity zinging its way to her bruised heart.

"Wait. I need to say something to you."

His hand dropped away as she turned back to him. Had he at last come to his senses and realized that what they had was worth fighting for?

The breath caught in her chest as she waited for his next words.

"I was a fool. I shouldn't have said those things to you in front of your sister. Please forgive me."

She nodded. "It's forgotten."

There had to be more. Anticipation had her stomach twisted in a knot. What was he waiting for? This was the part where they were supposed to kiss and make up. It's how it worked in the black-and-white romantic movies that she loved to watch late at night when she couldn't sleep.

"Do you want me to walk with you back to the villa? I can if you just give me a couple of minutes to finish filling out this form."

It wasn't going to happen. Their happy ending was not to be. She expelled a trapped breath and pulled her shoulders back. "No need. Finish what you were doing. I have some calls to make. I'll see you at dinner."

Her feet felt weighted down as she walked away. Since when had she become such a romantic? It wasn't good. Not good at all. She had to forget Stefano and her Roman holiday. In just a few days she'd catch her flight back to reality, but first she had to make sure this wedding went off without a hitch.

CHAPTER EIGHTEEN

ALL DECKED OUT in a new tux, Stefano stood at the altar.

He resisted the urge to pull at his collar. His brother stood next to him as the wedding music started to play. Dante had a permanent smile tattooed on his face. It was as it should be, but Stefano struggled to keep from frowning over the way he'd messed up with Jules.

He missed the gentle chime of her laughter. The way her eyes twinkled when she smiled.

Who was he kidding? He missed everything about her. She was so close and yet so far away. They were cordial to each other but nothing more. No teasing banter. No easy conversation.

Amid everything, Jules hadn't let it distract her. She had worked tirelessly from the time she got up until she called it a night. She'd been driven to make the wedding perfect. And it was amazing. She was amazing.

As though his thoughts had summoned her,

Jules started up the aisle between the rows of white chairs with purple bows. Guests dressed in their finest turned to watch her walk up the aisle. She looked absolutely stunning in a knee-length purple dress with a black sash accentuating her narrow waist. And the fitted bodice snuggled to her curves just perfectly while leaving the butterfly tattoo peeking over the top. Stefano stifled a groan of frustration. He forced his eyes upward, noticing how the strapless dress left a clear and enticing view of her sun-kissed shoulders. It was impossible for him to look away from her.

Jules didn't appear to have a similar problem. She kept her gaze straight forward. Was she purposely avoiding looking at him? Or was she nervous about standing in front of a large group of his extended family while television cameras were pointed at her from almost every angle?

She held her chin high. With her dark hair swept up, her slender neck was left exposed with only a gold chain adorning it. Stefano's mind meandered back in time to when they'd made love. He knew exactly where her ticklish spot was, right there in the gentle curve that sloped into her shoulder. He halted the tantalizing thought.

When she neared him, she glanced his way. He expected to find fury—or anger—at the very least pain, but there was no sign of those emotions reflected in her emerald eyes. That was good, right? She'd already gotten over him. So why didn't he feel relieved?

As she took her position opposite him, the guests rose to their feet as the wedding march played. Lizzie started down the aisle on the arm of Massimo. His grandfather had surprised everyone when he'd announced that he'd worked extra hard at his therapy so he could walk Lizzie down the aisle without the aid of his walker. Stefano wasn't sure who beamed brighter, the bride or Massimo. It seemed as though it was a day for happy endings…or beginnings, depending on how you looked at it.

When Lizzie joined hands with Dante, the minister cleared his throat. "Welcome. We are gathered today to celebrate the joining of two hearts…"

As the ceremony continued, Stefano became distracted by the smile on Jules's face. It lit up her eyes and made them sparkle like fine gems.

Even though he was happy for his brother, Stefano couldn't shake the dark cloud hanging over him. He knew what it was—it was Jules's impending departure. He'd been pretending that there was plenty of time to make peace between them before she left, but now the moment had arrived, and he didn't know what to say to make things better.

The minister clasped his hands together. "And

now the bride and groom will share the vows that they've written for each other."

Her hand in his, Lizzie peered up at Dante. "I never ever intended to fall in love with you. When we met, you were so stubborn and irritating." She smiled at him. Happiness danced in her eyes. "And did I mention stubborn?"

Dante's brows rose, but he didn't say a word as he continued to stare at his bride. Stefano's focus strayed back to Jules, whose eyes looked a bit misty as Lizzie continued to recite her vows.

"But then you showed me your patience, your generosity and your heart. It was then that I knew I'd at last found what I've been looking for my whole life—a home."

Stefano's heart leaped into his throat, blocking his breath. It was as though Lizzie had looked inside his heart and read his feelings for Jules. She was his home. How in the world was he going to live without the sound of her voice, the contagiousness of her laughter or the excitement he found in her kiss?

Stefano had no clue what his brother's vows were because the next thing Stefano knew the minister was saying, "And do you, Dante De-Fiore, take Elizabeth Addler to be your wife, to have and to hold, from this day forward, for better, for worse, for richer, for poorer, in sickness and health, as long as you both shall live?"

Without hesitation and in a loud, clear voice, Dante said, "I do."

The minister smiled. "I now pronounce you husband and wife. You may kiss the bride."

Dante didn't waste any time gathering his bride in his arms. A round of applause filled the air. If the heat of their first married kiss was any indication, it wouldn't be long until he was a proud, doting uncle. They made a great couple. And he couldn't be happier for them.

As the reception kicked off with tissue-paper flowers everywhere and upbeat music filling the air, Stefano stood off to the side. His gaze followed Jules around the dance floor. It appeared he wasn't the only one to notice her beauty. He'd swear every one of his male relatives had paid her a compliment or two. And the single ones were all lining up to dance with her.

He'd done nothing but think of her this past week to the point of his father chasing him out of the office after screwing up an order for an important customer. Stefano didn't make mistakes—well, he hadn't before Jules stepped into his life. Now he seemed to be making one after the other.

Jules truly was something special, and he'd let her get away because of his guilt over Gianna's death. He didn't think anything could wipe that memory away, but Jules might be right, too, that this self-imposed punishment wouldn't help Gianna or himself. Nothing would bring her or their baby back. It was time that he let the past rest and move forward. After all, there was plenty of room in his heart for both the past and the future.

Dante gestured to him from the side of the dance floor. What could his brother possibly want now? Stefano had smiled for all the pictures even though there wasn't an ounce of him that was in a jovial mood.

Like the dutiful best man, he made his way across the crowded dance floor, trying not to stare at Jules as his cousin Roberto held her a little too close. Stefano made a mental note to have a talk with his cousin later. Averting his gaze, it came to rest on Papa smiling broadly as he held Maria in his arms. It would seem that his father truly was giving love a second chance and in public for all the extended family to see.

"What do you need?" Stefano asked his brother.

"Have you forgotten that you're the best man?"

"No." His focus was drawn like a magnet to Jules, wishing that he was the one holding her close and that she was smiling up at him.

Dante shoved a champagne flute in his hand. "Stefano, did you hear anything I said?"

"What? Sorry I was distracted."

"So I noticed. Well, don't worry—you'll have your turn to dance with her soon."

"Really?" He realized too soon that he'd let

his anxiousness show, and that was not a good thing around his brother. He glanced over to see Dante laughing. Stefano frowned at him. "What's so funny?"

"You are, big brother. Looks like I better take some notes tonight about being the best man because you have it worse than I first thought—much worse."

Stefano turned away. He didn't like being the center of Dante's amusement, especially not when he knew that his time with Jules was severely limited.

"I'm not dancing with her." He wasn't going to torture himself. Standing here watching her in the arms of these other men was enough torture.

"Yes, you are. As soon as you give the toast."

He'd forgotten about the speech. He'd taken the time to write one out. He searched his pockets. The note card. It was missing. And the words escaped him.

"You do have the toast memorized, don't you? Because they're going to make an announcement as soon as this dance is over."

"Yes, I've got it." Stefano lied as he frantically searched his memory for what he'd been planning to say before he let himself get distracted.

The music stopped. Before he was ready a microphone was shoved in his hand. He cleared his throat and hoped he could think of a toast on his toes.

"Could I have everyone's attention?"

Silence fell over the crowd. He immediately spotted Jules. She was staring at him. His heart slammed into his chest, and his palms grew moist.

"I know you're all having fun, and I promise this won't take long. I'd introduce myself, but seeing as most of you are family, I'm guessing you already know my name. At least I hope you do." The audience laughed and a few hassled him.

"I'd like to take a moment and thank the maid of honor for her tireless effort to make this day perfect. Everyone, give Jules a hand." They gazed into each other's eyes as the applause rose.

"And now for the happy couple. Don't they just make the perfect pair?" Another round of applause filled the air, and the couple kissed. "Now, with me being the older brother, it's my responsibility to keep Dante on the right path, so I'm going to give him the only advice he'll ever need to maintain a happy marriage. Are you ready, Dante?"

Dante laughed and nodded. "Give it to me."

"Okay, repeat after me, 'Yes, dear.'"

"Yes, dear."

"There. You've got it. That's all you have to remember."

Lizzie smiled. "Very good." The guests laughed some more.

"And that is the extent of my knowledge about women. You're on your own for the rest of it, little brother. Now for the toast." He raised his glass. "To Lizzie, for never giving up on my brother. And to Dante, I don't know how you got so lucky, but you've gotten yourself a great lady. Never forget it. Here's hoping both of you have a lifetime of happiness."

In that moment, as his brother kissed his bride, a revelation came to Stefano. He realized that in all his effort to push Jules away, it hadn't been about her happiness. Sure, he wanted her to fulfill her dreams, but his inability to hear what she was telling him was due to the fact that if he let her into his heart, then she might later realize that he wasn't what she wanted. The thought of her rejecting him scared him senseless. He couldn't stand the thought of not being able to make her happy.

But as Dante looped his arm through his bride's so that they were linked as they sipped their bubbly, Stefano realized that love was a leap of faith. Without trust there could be no love. And he trusted Jules. Somewhere along the way he'd gotten to know the girl hiding behind all the makeup and funky clothes.

Life was full of risks. And life could change in

a heartbeat. If his father and brother were willing to put themselves out there, even though they knew the risks, what was he doing playing it safe and letting the woman he loved get away?

His mouth grew dry, and he took a sip of champagne. In the next moment, someone whisked the mic out of his hand. When he looked up, Jules was headed his way. His heart pounded, his pulse raced and his hands grew clammy.

This was his moment—his chance to win over the woman he loved. The thought didn't strike him as sudden or earth-shattering. Instead the acknowledgment came easily and calmly. It'd been growing over time, but he'd been doing everything to fight it.

Jules clenched her teeth tight as she forced a smile on her face. This was going to be the last time she was in Stefano's arms. She blinked rapidly. Now wasn't the time to get emotional.

All too soon, he stood before her. He was so tall that his gaze went over her head. She didn't know what to say to him. Did she try again to make him see sense? Or did she just let it go and accept that this wasn't going to happen for them?

Before she could make up her mind, a photographer was in her face snapping their picture. As they started to dance, she chanced a glance at Stefano, who surprisingly looked at ease. His smile made her heart flip-flop. Eventually he was going to make some woman a good husband. Too bad it wasn't going to be her.

"I've been wanting to talk to you." The sound of Stefano's voice startled her from her thoughts. "But you've been busy dancing."

"Yes. It's been nice, especially since I'll be stuck on a plane tomorrow."

"You've decided to go ahead with grad school?" When she nodded, it was like a light went out in his eyes. "I'm sure you'll be happy with the choice."

She shrugged. "We'll see. Anyway, I have to get back and find someplace cheap to live before classes start." When he adjusted his hold, her heart did a rapid *tap-tap-tap*. "What did you want to talk about?"

"Uh, nothing important. I just wanted to offer you a ride to the airport."

"Thanks, but I'm getting a lift with Dante and Lizzie."

"Have a safe trip home."

This was killing her. The last thing in the world she wanted to do was say goodbye to him. "Is that what you really want? Me to leave?"

They stopped dancing, and his hand lifted to her cheek. His long, lean fingers caressed her as he stared into her eyes. "I—"

A round of applause drew her attention. *What*

in the world? She looked around and realized the music had stopped a while ago and they were the only couple left on the dance floor. Heat rose in her cheeks. She didn't know if it was because she hadn't noticed the music stopping or if it was because she'd broken down once again and asked Stefano to change his mind about them.

But what she wanted to know more than anything was what he was about to say. "Say it. Say whatever it is."

"Come on, Jules! It's time for the bridal bouquet toss." Lizzie waved frantically to her from the other end of the dance floor, where a group of single females was anxiously waiting.

"Go. You are needed. We can talk about this later."

Later? How was she supposed to concentrate on anything until she knew what he was going to say? Her intuition told her that he was about to say he loved her. But was that just wishful thinking?

She walked closer to the group of excited young women. Their faces were all aglow with hopeful smiles, but there was nothing but turmoil lurking behind Jules's smile. The wedding may be in Italy, but Lizzie insisted on mixing traditions between those of Dante's family and what they were used to in New York. That had included the

Chicken Dance, which had succeeded in getting everyone laughing.

Catching the bridal bouquet was one tradition that Jules could do without. A happily-ever-after didn't appear to be in the cards for her. As if fate wanted to teach her a lesson, the bouquet of pink, orange and white blossoms landed squarely in her hands.

While everyone clapped, her gaze strayed to Stefano. He wasn't clapping, but he was staring directly at her. She wished she could read his mind.

CHAPTER NINETEEN

STEFANO'S HEART SLAMMED into his chest as he stared at Jules's holding the bridal bouquet. She stared right back at him.

She was trying to tell him something, but what? He had to get this right. He couldn't afford to make any more mistakes.

Had she forgiven him? Was she willing to give him another chance? *Live in the moment*—her words echoed through his mind. He needed to trust her and her decisions—no matter what direction they led her. Although he prayed that it would be toward him.

Stefano straightened his shoulders. This had been put off long enough. He would let her know that he loved her and then he'd accept whatever decision she made.

He started toward her only to have her pulled aside for more wedding photos, this time holding the bridal bouquet. There was no way he was intruding on that moment. He'd had enough photos of himself taken to last him the rest of his life. But he also wasn't letting her out of his sight.

He didn't know how much time passed as he talked to one distant relative after the other—some he didn't even recall their names and had to fake it. And every time he was free, Jules was having more photos taken or being escorted around the dance floor. Even his father had taken his turn dancing with her.

"What are you waiting for, boy?"

He turned to find Nonno behind him. His grandfather's gaze moved from him to Jules, who was getting a drink of punch. How did his grandfather know what he was waiting to say? Was it that obvious?

"I…I didn't want to bother her."

With the aid of a walker, his grandfather moved next to him and lowered his voice. "You aren't going to bother her. I've seen the way she looks at you. Don't let her get away."

"You…you think she'll want me after I messed up?" His grandfather nodded and Stefano added, "Thanks, Nonno."

"Go. Be happy."

Jules didn't see him approaching, and she started to walk in the opposite direction. He wasn't going to turn back, not until he got this off his chest. He continued following and inwardly groaned when she approached Dante and Lizzie.

The last thing he wanted to do was lay his heart on the line in front of his brother. There had to be a better way, but he was running out of time. Determined not to lose his chance, he continued over and joined the small group. They were deep in conversation.

Jules looked directly at her sister. "I wanted to let you two know that I won't need a ride tomorrow morning to the airport."

"What?" Lizzie's eyes opened wide. "But why not?"

"You know I love you." Jules's tone was low and firm. "And I know that if it wasn't for you I wouldn't be standing here. You've been the most amazing sister, but there's something I've been trying to tell you. For one reason or another it was never the right time. I'm beginning to think there'll never be a right time, so I'm just going to say it."

No one moved. Stefano wasn't even sure that Lizzie breathed as she stood transfixed on her sister. Mentally he urged Jules onward. It was finally time that she spoke up for herself.

"It's past time I start making my own decisions and for you to respect them."

Lizzie sent her a worried look. "I have a feeling I'm not going to like this."

"Probably not. But here it goes, anyway. I'm not going to grad school." Lizzie opened her mouth, but Jules held up her palm, silencing her. "I know that you already paid the tuition. Whatever isn't refundable, I'll pay you back."

Lizzie looked more stunned than upset. "But why? I thought this is what you wanted—to help the kids like us."

"I do. But social work isn't for me." Jules glanced down and wiggled her sandaled foot on the floor. "The thing is I can't follow all of their rules all of the time. Sometimes they just don't make sense. And, well, I spoke up one too many times, and they let me go from my internship early."

"Oh. Jules, I'm sorry. But that doesn't mean—"

"It means that I wasn't happy there. And I will find another way to help less fortunate children. I already have some ideas."

Concern creased Lizzie's face. "I...I don't know what to say. Are you sure about this?"

"I'm absolutely certain. This isn't a decision I made lightly. I've thought about it for a long time."

"Then I guess there isn't anything else to say, except I love you. And I'm here if you need me."

They hugged. And though everyone else wore serious expressions, Stefano couldn't help but smile—his first genuine smile that day. He was so happy for Jules to speak up for herself. Now it was time that he did the same thing. Whether his brother witnessed his groveling or not, he was speaking his heart, here and now.

He cleared his throat. "Jules, can I speak with you?"

She spun around, and her expression was perfectly serious. "Not before I have my say." She pointed a finger at him. "And I've made a decision about you." She poked at his chest. "I've decided that you are stubborn and irritating, but that I love you, anyway. And I'm not giving up on you because I think you love me, too."

The way she gazed at him, it was as if she could read his every thought. And though not so long ago that would have scared him, now he found comfort in someone knowing him so well.

Stefano wrapped his hand around hers and pressed her palm to his pounding chest. "Thank you for being so insistent and giving me a chance to come to my senses because I do love you. I love you with all my heart."

"You do?"

"I do."

She smiled broadly. "Just remember those words because you'll be saying them again soon."

"I can't wait." He could already envision their future, and it was going to be a happy one. He'd never again become disconnected. He'd make Jules's happiness and their marriage his top priority.

Jules leaned up on her tiptoes as he leaned down. Their lips met in the middle. The empty spot in his heart flooded with love. He wrapped his arms around her and swung her around in a circle. He never planned to let her go.

EPILOGUE

One year later...

"IT'S OFFICIAL."

Jules smiled up at her very sexy husband and gave off a squeal of excitement. The noise of the family picnic in the background covered up her excitement. She'd never been so happy in her life. She almost had everything she wanted. Almost...

Stefano gathered her in his arms and swung her around as his lips pressed to hers. It didn't matter how many times he kissed her, her heart still fluttered with excitement.

"And what's going on over here?"

Stefano set her feet back on the ground. She straightened her purple top and black miniskirt. When she glanced up she found Lizzie looking expectantly at both of them as she rested a hand over her expanding midsection.

"Your sister is now an official Italian citizen," Stefano said proudly.

"Is that so?" Lizzie radiated with a motherly glow. "Well, if you two aren't careful with the celebrating, you'll end up like me. Swollen ankles. And a backache to boot."

"And you look so miserable," Jules teased her, knowing full well that Lizzie was absolutely thrilled with her handsome husband and their impending bundle of joy.

"What can I say? I'm deliriously in love." Lizzie grinned.

"Are you talking about me?" Dante sauntered up and put an arm around his wife's expanding waist, pulling her close.

"Don't worry," Jules spoke up. "We've got an announcement to make, too."

Lizzie straightened. Her eyes widened. "Jules, are you preggers?"

She shook her head, sending her pigtails swishing back and forth. Both Dante and Lizzie sent her a puzzled look. When she just grinned at them, they turned to Stefano for answers.

He smiled and shrugged. "She'll tell you."

"Well, tell us—we're dying to know."

Stefano's arms slipped over her shoulders. She loved the feel of him next to her. He was her best friend. Her lover. Her soul mate. With him by her side anything was possible.

"We're going to be parents, too."

Lizzie's forehead wrinkled. "But you said you aren't pregnant."

"I'm not. We're going to adopt some of the older kids that need a loving home. We have this big place and think it would be nice to share it with some children that don't have a home."

Lizzie's eyes filled with tears. "You found a way to help kids like us, after all. You are amazing. Both of you are amazing."

Jules gazed lovingly into her husband's eyes. They were amazing together. And Jules couldn't think of anything better than living and working next to Dante while opening their hearts and home to some less fortunate children. Their journey was just beginning, and she knew that it wouldn't be all roses. There'd be a few thorns along the way, but together they'd work their way past them.

* * * * *

This is the second story
in Jennifer Faye's fabulous
THE DeFIORE BROTHERS DUET.
The first in the duet,
THE PLAYBOY OF ROME,
is already available—don't miss it!

LARGER-PRINT BOOKS!

GET 2 FREE LARGER-PRINT NOVELS PLUS
2 FREE GIFTS!

⊕ HARLEQUIN®

Romance

From the Heart, For the Heart

One night with her husband can't hurt Jessica, can it…?
Unless it has dramatic, life-changing consequences!

Read on for a sneak preview of
THE PREGNANCY SECRET
by **Cara Colter**

"I'm not divorcing you," Jessica said. "We're divorcing each other. Isn't that what you want?"

Kade found where her sling was discarded on the floor and looped it gently over her head.

"It seems to be what you want, all of a sudden," he said. "There's something you aren't telling me, isn't there?"

She felt suddenly weak, as if she could blurt out her deepest secret to him. How would it feel to tell him? *Kade, there is going to be a baby after all.*

No, that was not the type of thing to blurt out. What would be her motivation? Did she think it would change things between them? She didn't want them to change because of a baby. She wanted them to change because he loved her.

What? She didn't want things to change between them at all. She was taking steps to close this door, not reopen it! She was happy.

"Happy, happy, happy," she muttered out loud.

"Huh?"

"Oh. Just thinking out loud."

He looked baffled, as well he should!

"Go to bed," he told her. "We'll talk later. Now is obviously not the time."

He had that right! Where were these thoughts coming from? She needed to get her defenses back up.

With what seemed to be exquisite tenderness, he slipped her cast back inside the sling, adjusted the knot on the back of her neck.

His touch made her feel hungry for him and miss him more than it seemed possible. He put his hand on her left elbow and helped her up, and then across the bathroom and into the bedroom.

He let go of her only long enough to turn back the bedclothes and help her slide into the bed.

He tucked the covers up around her and stood looking down at her.

"Okay," she said, "I'm fine. You can leave."

He started to go, but then he turned back and stood in the bedroom door, one big shoulder braced against the frame.

He looked at her long and hard, until the ache came back so strong she had to clamp her teeth together to keep herself from flicking open the covers, an invitation.

Don't miss
THE PREGNANCY SECRET by Cara Colter,
available May 2015 wherever
Harlequin® Romance books and ebooks are sold.

www.Harlequin.com

HREXP0415